CANDLE FACE CHRONICLES

THE LOST SOULS
[BOOK ONE]

Arthur Mills

CANDLE FACE CHRONICLES

THE LOST SOULS
[BOOK ONE]

ARTHUR MILLS

Branching Plot Books

2024

ISBN: Paperback   978-1-7363392-2-0
            eBook for Kindle   978-1-7363392-3-7

BOOKS BY ARTHUR MILLS

- The Empty Lot Next Door
- The Crawl Space
- Friend or Foe
- Co-Author
- Candle Face Chronicles: The Lost Souls [Book One]
- Candle Face Chronicles: The Lost Souls [Book Two]
- Candle Face Chronicles: Isabel: The Forgotten Daughter of La Llorona [Book Three]
- The Haunted Handbook
- The Legend of Mara Flores

DEDICATION

This book is for my readers, the ones willing to look closer.

The Lost Souls came to me because they want two things: for their remains to be found and for the people who killed them to be identified. Their stories were cut short by betrayal, violence, and fear, but they haven't gone silent.

As you read, pay attention to the details. A road, a name, a job, a family tie, a habit, or a final conversation may be the clue that breaks a case open. If you catch something I missed, follow it. Bring it to candleface.com and help me solve these cases.

You're part of this investigation now.

THE LOST SOULS

Candle Face, her visage scarred by fire,

Hunts the skeptics, fueled by ire.

Each disbeliever, a soul to claim,

Trapped forever in her game.

She drifts through darkness, ghostly pale,

Her wrath a silent, haunting wail.

Lost souls speak of their fate,

Caught in her grasp, they relate.

In the shadows, their voices blend,

"The Lost Souls" cry, without end.

KEY TO UNDERSTANDING

To fully understand this book, readers should be familiar with my memoir *The Empty Lot Next Door*, which was inspired by actual ghostly events in Austin, Texas. That book gives readers the background needed to understand the events and references that shape *Candle Face Chronicles: The Lost Souls [Book One]*. Without that context, some parts of this book may not have the same impact. For that reason, reading *The Empty Lot Next Door* first is strongly recommended.

To purchase *The Empty Lot Next Door*, please visit Amazon

- Paperback: https://amzn.to/46lCovb
- eBook for Kindle: https://amzn.to/44YFww4
- Audiobook for Audible: https://amzn.to/40RIHH1

GUIDING QUESTIONS FOR THE LOST SOULS

As you read each testimony, slow down and look for details that can be checked. Start with these questions:

1. What names, nicknames, dates, roads, landmarks, jobs, ages, habits, or family details might help identify the spirit?

2. What in the testimony may point to where the person died, disappeared, or was left?

3. Who had power over the spirit in life? Look closely at friends, partners, relatives, coworkers, followers, and anyone who may have betrayed, pressured, or lured them.

4. What does this testimony add to the pattern? Pay attention to how Candle Face appears, what she says, what her followers do, and how belief, doubt, or refusal is used against the victim.

5. What detail should be checked next? Compare it with earlier testimonies, look for repeated names or locations, and share anything useful at candleface.com.

Research carefully. The Lost Souls are depending on you.

TABLE OF CONTENTS

INTRODUCTION

When I was growing up on the haunted stretch of Ben Howell Drive in Austin, Texas, during the wild 1970s and 1980s, I came into contact with a presence that changed my life. I called her Candle Face because of her charred features. My battles with her, both physical and spiritual, started in my youth and ended with what I believed was her banishment back to the hell she came from. I was wrong. That victory didn't last, and her story was far from over.

While serving in the Army, I wrote my memoir, *The Empty Lot Next Door*, in 2010, hoping to put that part of my life behind me. When I retired and returned to Texas in 2021, I learned Candle Face had never been dormant.

In October 2023, I began an investigation to determine who or what she had been before I first encountered her in the mid-70s. What I found was disturbing. Candle Face had never been a product of my childhood imagination. She was a relentless force that targeted anyone who dared to deny her existence.

As I dug further into her history, anguished voices began to haunt me at night. They were the voices of her victims. Candle Face's followers had killed many people, and now these Lost Souls reach out from unmarked graves, pleading for justice and peace. At first, I resisted the idea of acting as their spokesperson, but it became clear that I was supposed to share their stories. My own history with Candle Face, years of writing, and decades spent in intelligence analysis and investigations put me in a position to take on that responsibility.

Accepting that role wasn't easy. Even after thirty years as an intelligence analyst and private investigator specializing in missing persons and human trafficking, the world of restless spirits was unlike anything I had faced.

That's why I'm reaching out to you, my readers. Together, we can help these Lost Souls. Your willingness to study the evidence is essential. Each chapter in this book is an account of one of Candle Face's victims and a call to act.

We're partners in finding the remains of these Lost Souls, identifying those responsible for their deaths, and, if possible, ending Candle Face's power over them. The spirits chose me to carry their cries for help, but I can't do this alone.

These journal entries invite you into an unusual investigation. By piecing together each victim's life, locating hidden graves, and identifying their killers, we're working cold cases while giving troubled spirits a chance at peace.

Maybe, if we stand together and keep going, we'll confront Candle Face once more. This time, we may be able to make sure she never returns.

As an investigator, I know the value of a journal. Details fade. Patterns get missed. A name, a road, a phrase, or a date that seems minor in the moment can later become the key to identifying a victim, locating remains, or understanding a killer. What follows is drawn from the journal I kept as these events unfolded. I've gathered those entries here because this investigation is bigger than one person, and having more eyes on these accounts gives us a better chance of helping the Lost Souls and understanding Candle Face.

A RESEARCH PROJECT DERAILED

October 12, 2023

Returning to Texas pushed me to find out who Candle Face really is. She's the 11-year-old ghost girl from *The Empty Lot Next Door*, the presence that haunted my childhood, in nightmares and in daylight, with her melted, disfigured face.

But she didn't stop with me. Over the years, other Austin residents shared their own frightening encounters. Many sent letters, which I had set aside for future research. Now, with renewed focus, I've gone back to that file.

Almost immediately, the investigation took a bad turn. Two of the three original witnesses I contacted have vanished. They stopped returning calls and emails. The third had once been eager to talk, but after a threatening dream about Candle Face, he backed out without warning. He described what she said to him and decided silence was the safer choice.

Their stories have gone quiet for now. If any of them decide to come forward again, I'll go to Austin without hesitation to document and share what they know.

At this point, the investigation feels stalled. I'm sorting through scattered leads, moving carefully through Candle Face's history, and trying not to get trapped in the same dead ends that stopped others before me.

AN ELDERLY WITNESS TO CANDLE FACE'S PAST

October 29, 2023

In an unexpected development, the elderly gentleman who once avoided my attempts to interview him has changed his mind. Our long-delayed meeting is finally set for later today.

At 82, he carries memories from a time most people have long since forgotten. He says he knew Candle Face before I ever encountered her or gave her that name, and that he watched parts of her story play out.

For years, he kept what he knew to himself. Now he's chosen to speak, despite the risk. By sharing what he remembers, he may be putting himself in danger.

I can't help but wonder what he'll tell me. How did his life cross paths with Candle Face before the fire that left her with those melted features?

As the interview gets closer, I can feel it bearing down on me. I may be about to hear a story from someone who was there long before the world knew she existed.

A WITNESS SPEAKS ABOUT CANDLE FACE

October 31, 2023

I tracked down an 82-year-old man with firsthand knowledge of the tragic fire on Ben Howell Drive in Austin, Texas. For his safety and privacy, he asked to be identified as Mr. John Doe and insisted on complete anonymity before sharing his story.

The following pages contain the transcript of our brief but intense interview. We had only ten minutes to cover events that stretched back decades, so every question had to count. In that short time, Mr. Doe gave me new information about the fire and described his own encounter with the ghost I've come to call Candle Face.

Interview date: October 30, 2023
Location: Austin, Texas

Arthur: Mr. Doe, did you live near Ben Howell Drive in the 1960s or 1970s?

John Doe: Yes. My family lived close to Ben Howell Drive. We were there from around the mid-1960s into the mid-1980s. We left after the kids were grown and married.

Arthur: There was a bad fire on Ben Howell in the late 1960s. Do you remember it?

John Doe: I do. The father was cleaning a carburetor in the kitchen with gasoline. One of the boys knocked over the gas can while the mother was cooking. Gas spilled, the fumes caught, and the whole place went up fast. There were several children in the house. They got out, but they were badly burned. The father couldn't find his youngest son, who was about two years old. He thought the boy had run back inside. His wife and his mother went in too, but the fire pushed them back out. The father tried to go in again, but people held him back. When the firefighters first searched the house, they didn't find the boy. Everybody thought he had wandered off, so people started searching the neighborhood and calling his name. I think his name was Paul, but I can't say for sure. Later, they found his body in the kitchen.

Arthur: Do you remember anything else from that night?

John Doe: I remember the mother sitting on the curb across the street, crying her eyes out, with neighbors around her. I also remember the father getting arrested that same night. From what I heard, it was for a parole violation that had nothing to do with the fire. I always thought that was cold. His family was hurt, and his little boy had just died.

Arthur: You said the child's name may have been Paul. Do you know if one of the other children was named Griffin?

John Doe: No, not that I know of. I remember hearing Paul. I don't remember Griffin.

Arthur: As you know, I moved next door to the empty lot where that house once stood. I heard stories growing up about what happened there.

John Doe: What stories?

Arthur: When we moved there in 1976, I was only four. The neighborhood kids told me the little boy had caused the fire by playing with matches near the water heater. They also said the whole family died and got buried in the backyard because they couldn't afford plots in a cemetery.

John Doe: [Laughs] That sounds like something kids would make up. No, that isn't what happened. There were no backyard burials, and the whole family didn't die. Only the little boy died in the fire. I remember reading that part in your book and getting a laugh out of it.

Arthur: In my book, *The Empty Lot Next Door*, I wrote about dreams I had of a little girl coming up out of a hole in the back of the lot.

John Doe: [Laughs again] I remember the hole. But why would she come out of a hole?

Arthur: I wondered if it might have been an old septic tank that caved in.

CANDLE FACE CHRONICLES: THE LOST SOULS [BOOK ONE]

John Doe: No. Houses over there didn't use septic tanks. It was probably just a hole. I wouldn't get carried away with it.

Arthur: I used to stand around that hole with the other kids. One of the older boys, Randy, dared somebody to jump in and said the ghost of a little girl would haunt whoever did it. One evening, I jumped in. After that, I started dreaming about a little girl with a burned face. Later, she left handprints on my windows. To me, that proved she was real.

John Doe: But you don't know she was buried there. Why did you jump in?

Arthur: I was the smallest kid around, and I was tired of being overlooked. I wanted to do something that made me stand out on my own, outside my brother Ricky's shadow.

John Doe: Well, whatever the reason, maybe you woke something up. I don't think she was buried there. Maybe it was some kind of portal. But you're the investigator, not me.

Arthur: If it were some kind of portal, do you think it could be closed?

John Doe: You're making it sound like a movie.

Arthur: Mr. Doe, do you believe in Candle Face?

John Doe: Yes. It's better to believe, just in case. It's akin to an insurance policy. If you believe, you're safe. If not, you might end up with a visit.

Arthur: How do you know that? Why do you think she goes after people who don't believe?

John Doe: I've heard stories over the years. People say she goes after skeptics, especially people living rough or making bad choices, though not always. Some decent people have had run-ins too. I can't explain all that. I just know what I heard, and I know what I saw myself.

Arthur: You saw her?

John Doe: Yes. Around 1990, I was walking my dog near that creek you wrote about, by Wilson and El Paso streets. I saw a young girl in the water. She had long dark hair and looked like she was bathing or washing off. She looked up at me, and we locked eyes. I kept trying to get a better look. I thought I heard a voice say, "Do you believe?" Maybe it was the wind. Maybe it wasn't. I said yes, as quietly as I could, just in case. She went back to what she was doing. I never saw her again. Later, I heard other stories about a little girl ghost, though people didn't call her Candle Face. I believed it was the same one.

Arthur: Do you think Candle Face is still out there?

John Doe: Yes, I do.

Arthur: In July, when we spoke on the phone, you said you had information about Candle Face from before I awakened her. What did you mean?

John Doe: I meant I saw her in 1990, long before you wrote your book. I didn't know you back then. I didn't know your story. That's all I meant.

Arthur: Do you think anyone else from the neighborhood may have seen her or heard stories about her?

John Doe: Probably. I know a few people who might know

something. Most are my age. A couple are closer to yours. But I don't know if they would talk.

Arthur: Why not?

John Doe: Because some of them don't believe. And even if they say they don't believe, they're still scared.

Arthur: If they don't believe, then maybe they don't have anything to worry about.

John Doe: That's not how fear works. You can still be scared even if you don't believe. Maybe especially then. But I'm not asking around for you. That's your job.

Arthur: Fair enough. Is there anything else you want to add?

John Doe: Just be careful. You may find what you're looking for. And if you do, remember what I told you. Belief may be its own kind of insurance.

Arthur: Thank you for your time, Mr. Doe.

The interview with Mr. John Doe provided useful information, especially about the fire and what people were already saying about it. As I continue looking into her past, I keep returning to Shakespeare's line: "There are more things in heaven and earth, Horatio, than are dreamt of in your philosophy." My effort to understand Candle Face continues, and so does the feeling that some parts of it remain outside what I can explain.

GENESIS: THE NIGHTMARES

November 4, 2023

Every night, as the world sleeps, my sense of reality starts to come apart. It's been four days since these strange, almost psychedelic states began, and each one feels disturbingly familiar, like a terrifying déjà vu I can't escape. Falling asleep now feels like stepping into something I don't fully understand, where closing my eyes opens the door to something haunting.

It all started quietly enough on the night after my interview with Mr. Doe. Our conversation centered on a grim truth: the tragic story of a house fire in 1969. He described the little boy lost in the flames with a vividness that left me uncomfortable. Despite the room's chill, I felt a strange warmth creeping in as he detailed the charred remains of what had once been a cheerful home and the stories of Candle Face.

As I reflected on his account, my thoughts kept returning to the hole at the back of the empty lot, the one my friends and I dared each other to jump into as children. I had always associated Candle Face with that spot, perhaps because of the vivid dreams I had after standing in it. While Mr. Doe didn't confirm its significance, he speculated that it might have been a portal of some kind, not a burial site.

The night after we spoke, I sensed a shift, as if his words had stirred something dormant. As I lay in bed, the blackness behind my eyelids filled with swirling colors that shifted and pulsed. It felt like I was being shown something, or warned.

Then came the voices, a chaotic mix of shouting and screams. Their words were garbled, but their tone was unmistakable: anger, urgency, confusion. The sensation held me somewhere between waking and sleeping, weightless and on edge, as if I might drift away at any moment.

Each night since, the sequence has replayed. I jolt awake, heart pounding, only to face the same cycle when I try to sleep again. By day, I tell myself it's stress or an overactive imagination, but deep down, I know these episodes are tied to Mr. Doe's story.

By the fourth night, exhaustion had set in. I scoured online forums, desperate for answers, and stumbled across "hypnagogic hallucinations," vivid experiences between waking and sleeping. The descriptions fit, but they didn't explain why my dreams mirrored Mr. Doe's story so clearly: the little boy, the fire, and Candle Face.

I kept replaying his words. He spoke of Candle Face with conviction, calling her a spirit who punishes those who mock her. Had his belief seeped into my subconscious and shaped these dreams?

Desperate, I reached out to Mr. Doe again. It was just as hard to reach him this time, and when I finally did, his response was, "Perhaps she's trying to tell you something." It wasn't the reassurance I'd hoped for. If anything, it confirmed my fear that these dreams might be more than hallucinations. Years ago, I disturbed Candle Face by trespassing into her resting place. Could my renewed investigation have drawn her attention again?

Tonight, as I prepare for bed, I'm caught between wanting answers and dreading another sleepless night. I've taken to sleeping with a light on, hoping it keeps the darkness, and the unease, at bay. If I can understand these nightly visits, maybe I can gain some control over them or stop them altogether. Until then, I remain stuck in this strange limbo between waking and sleeping, searching for some way through it.

Personal Note to My Readers

I'm longing for a full night of sleep that isn't overtaken by these vivid visions. The toll of these sleepless nights is wearing on my days and straining my work and relationships. It feels like the moment I started asking questions about Candle Face again, I pulled her back into my life, and now she won't let go.

My military training taught me to run toward a threat, not away from it. So I'm prepared to confront Candle Face. It's frightening, but I won't back down.

I know this could be a long road, with more nights of little or no sleep. Still, I'm committed. I hope that by facing whatever is behind these visions, I can finally sleep through the night again. I'm ready to see this through, no matter where it leads.

THE VOICES GROW STRONGER

November 8, 2023

It's been just over a week since the first strange, vivid dream, and I still feel trapped. What started as a blur of screams and shouts has grown into distinct voices, each one clearer and more insistent than before. They sound like people from every age and every kind of background, and they all seem to want the same thing. They're trying to speak to me.

I've read far too much about hypnagogic hallucinations, the term that first seemed to explain what was happening to me. But as the voices have sharpened and grown more demanding, I can't convince myself that stress alone explains it.

At first, all I saw were swirling patterns when I closed my eyes. Then the voices started coming through, as though those shifting shapes had opened a door. Now the sounds are constant, a chaotic mix of chatter, cries, and sobs. Some voices speak in languages I don't understand. Others are painfully clear. What's obvious is that they're trying to reach me.

Night after night, I struggle through it, only to wake up drenched in sweat, heart racing, with no relief waiting for me. I keep asking myself whether this connects to my research into Candle Face. By digging into her story, did I open some kind of portal? Is that what brought on this flood of voices?

I called Mr. Doe again to see whether he had any advice. His response was worse than I expected. "You must listen. They have chosen you for a reason." Then he hung up and told me to leave him alone.

That line, "They have chosen you," haunts me. Why me? I don't know. What does seem clear is that I'm not dealing with this by myself. Something else is tied up in it, and it isn't letting go.

As the nights drag on, I've started to separate individual voices from the chaos. Some sound like frightened children. Others carry bitterness and regret. The older voices carry a sorrow I can feel but still don't fully understand. They call me by my childhood name, Ray, and feed me pieces of their stories, conflicts left unsolved, lives ended too soon. They seem to believe I'm their chance to be heard.

The thought of becoming their messenger scares me. I want these voices gone so I can sleep. But each night they get louder, pushing me toward a choice I'm not ready to make. Leaving a light on no longer helps. The glow does nothing to keep this away. Whatever this is, it's getting stronger.

I'm torn between the urge to understand what's happening and the fear of what I might find if I fully open myself to their pleas. For now, I'm taking it one night at a time and writing everything down in the hope that it'll make sense later. Something in all of this points back to Candle Face, even if I can't yet explain how. Until I figure it out, I'm doing my best to hold on to my sanity.

Personal Note to My Readers

I never asked for these visits. My first instinct has been to shut out the details when I wake up, leaving behind only flashes of dread and confusion. Maybe that's instinct. Maybe it's a defense against what scares us most. But forgetting isn't an option this time. I didn't choose this, but it's happening anyway. Whether I like it or not, I'm in it now.

CANDLE FACE VICTIM #1: A SPIRIT BEGS TO DIE

November 12, 2023

My nightmares have not let up. The voices are getting clearer, and their stories are starting to make more sense. It's hard to admit, but I'm no longer sure I can keep ignoring them. I feel pulled deeper into this nightmare because I need to understand what they want from me and how it connects to Candle Face.

My dreams have changed, and I remember them more clearly now. I'm no longer watching from a distance. I'm in them, whether I want to be or not. As I drift between waking and sleep, I keep hoping I'll eventually understand what these voices are trying to tell me.

Then last night, something happened that jolted me awake. The dream was so vivid that I reached for a pen the moment I opened my eyes. In it, a spirit came to me and stood around my bed. She was different from the others. She was one voice, and she had a story she wanted heard.

As I listened, unable to look away, she told me she was one of Candle Face's victims. She never gave me her name, but she begged me to remember what had happened to her so it wouldn't be lost. Her words came through with a painful clarity that cut through the rest of the voices. This is what she said:

I hate life. I hate people. And most of all, I hate myself. Everyone and everything has been against me from the very beginning. Parents, siblings, friends, schools, the government, everyone, and everything else are against me. I want out of this world, this life of mine. I could end it myself, of course. I've tried many times, but somehow, I survived. I know ending my own life would mean heaven wouldn't take me, and I think hell wouldn't want me either.

A few years before Candle Face kidnapped me, I had hoped I wouldn't wake from surgery, but I did. I cried when I woke. I even ripped open the stitches above my own heart, hoping my heart would fall out. I wished for death many times, but my body kept betraying me. My own body wants me to continue being tormented by life. Why? Why must I constantly be tormented?

Candle Face explained it to me when she took me to her lair. She said my punishment for losing my faith in her would be eternal life with pain that would compound over time with each of her kills.

I'm not dead, I know. She keeps me alive just to torture me.

Will you help me? Ray, please help me die.

Hearing her felt like finding the missing piece that tied these dreams to Candle Face in a way I could no longer dismiss. Her plea left no doubt.

Not long ago, I said I wanted no part of this, even though I had little choice. Now I'm starting to think that if I can help these Lost Souls find peace, I may have to face this more directly than I wanted to.

Personal Note to My Readers

You should understand that the order of victims in *Candle Face Chronicles: The Lost Souls* may not match the order in which Candle Face killed them. I'm presenting them in the order they came to me and shared their experiences.

CANDLE FACE VICTIM #2: MAMA'S LAST EMBRACE

November 18, 2023

Last night, I had another visitor. A dark shape appeared near my bed just as I was drifting off to sleep. Little by little, it came into focus, and I realized someone else had come through. Standing only a few feet away was a young Black girl who looked about four or five years old. She seemed more frightened of me than I was of her. Tears ran down her cheeks as she pleaded for my help. She had a story to tell:

I remember the day I last saw my Mama. I was playing outside our mobile home, and it was really, really cold. The wind went whoosh against my cheeks. But the sky was blue, and the sun was low.

I sat there all bundled up in my winter coat, playing with my teddy bear that my Granny made for me. My teddy was dirty and fuzzy, but I loved it so much.

Then I saw some big kids playing near our mobile home. They were standing in a circle, and one of them, a big boy with nappy hair, was telling a scary story. He said there was a girl ghost around here who died in a fire, and now she scares kids who don't believe in her. The other kids listened with big eyes, all excited, even the tough ones.

But my Mama didn't like those stories. She came out of our home fast and waved her hands like she was mad. "Stop scaring my baby girl with those stories!" she yelled. One of the ladies with the kids said maybe we should believe just in case, but Mama was like, "Nope, my baby girl won't believe in silly stuff like that."

After Mama helped me brush my teeth that night, she tucked me into bed with my teddy. I felt safe and warm under the covers. Mama leaned in close and said, "Those ghost stories aren't real, sweetie. Grown-ups sometimes make them up to make kids behave."

I believed her because Mama knew everything and could protect me from anything. But that night, something strange happened.

I felt hot and heard a sizzling sound like bacon in a frying pan. My heart went boom boom really fast. Something hot picked me up, and it smelled bad, like burned cookies. I wanted to scream for Mama, but I couldn't. I was so scared.

Then Mama appeared. She was strong and loving, and she held me tight. She said it was just a bad dream and not real. I cried and told her about the ghost girl, but Mama said those stories couldn't hurt good girls who didn't believe in them.

Her words felt warm, and I fell asleep without any more bad dreams.

The next day, I heard a little cry while I was swinging on our swing in front of our mobile home. Mama was inside by the window, watching me. I heard something in the bushes. My heart started beating fast because I wanted to know what it was, but I was scared too.

When Mama moved away from the window, I went to look. I had hoped to find a hurt puppy, but instead I found a girl. Her skin was burned, and her clothes were torn. She looked so sad. I wanted to scream and run to Mama, but I couldn't. I was too scared.

I don't remember much after that. But I'm not with Mama and Granny anymore. I'm in a strange place with other kids and grown-ups who went through bad things too. I'm scared here. I don't like it.

I wish I could hug Mama and Granny one more time and feel their love and protection. Maybe you can find them one day and let them know I miss them.

The little girl gave me a grateful smile, though the sorrow in her eyes was hard to miss. As she backed toward the wall, her features began to fade until she was only a shadow, and then she was gone into the portal.

A rush of adrenaline hit me. I got out of bed and hurried downstairs as if something was pushing me forward. When I reached my computer, I typed as fast as I could, trying to capture every word she had shared before any of it slipped away.

These nighttime encounters make more sense now. Each visitor has carried the same plea. They're trapped by the spirit known as Candle Face, and they need my help. I never asked for this responsibility, but I don't seem to have a way around it. My job now is to document these encounters and bear witness to their stories. I don't know where any of this leads. At this point, almost everything is still uncertain.

Personal Note to My Readers

This visitor left more clues than I first realized. She appeared to be around four or five years old, African American, with short braids, possibly black and white, though that may have been the way the light caught her hair. Her voice was gentle, but she spoke in rushed bursts and kept glancing over her shoulder as if danger was close.

She didn't name her hometown, but the mention of Candle Face points to Austin, Texas, in winter. She said she lived in a mobile home with her mother and grandmother and called them "Mama" and "Granny." There was a swing set outside their home, and I suspect her last moment with her mother happened while she was playing on that swing.

These details may help identify her and explain what happened

If you want to help solve this and give this little girl the peace she deserves, join the investigation. You can share your findings and thoughts here: www.candleface.com.

CANDLE FACE VICTIM #3: SIXTH STREET TO THE GRAVEL PIT

November 23, 2023

Just before I fell asleep last night, I sensed another presence. This time there were two, a man and a woman, standing in the shadowed corner of my room with their faces half-hidden by the low light.

The man spoke first and asked for my help. They wanted me to be their voice, to tell how their lives ended and who killed them. As they spoke, their memories came together into one account of what happened to them. This is what they said:

> I traveled to Austin with my girlfriend to visit a childhood friend. As soon as we got to his house, we decided to go out and take in the nightlife on Sixth Street. The bars, the music, the energy, it was everything you would expect. We moved

from bar to bar, drinking, laughing, and taking it all in.

By the time we got back to my friend's house, we weren't ready to end the night. We ended up in his kitchen, opening more beers, and my friend passed around some weed. We were buzzed and in a good mood, at least until he started talking about a "presence" that haunted his house.

"She comes with rattling chains," he said.

My girlfriend and I looked at each other, barely holding back our laughter. "Rattling chains? Seriously?" she chuckled. "That's straight out of a bad horror movie."

"Exactly," I said, grinning. "Ghosts are just a product of imagination."

But my friend wasn't laughing. He got serious, and that only made us laugh harder.

"I might have exaggerated," he said, his voice turning somber, "but she visits me in my dreams. She asks for help. She asks me to find people who believe in her."

I raised an eyebrow. "What do you mean, believe?"

He hesitated, then described the dreams, a disfigured little girl trying to communicate with him. At first, he couldn't understand her, but over time, her words became clearer.

"I'm out," my girlfriend said, standing up. "This is too much."

"What's wrong?" he asked. "Are you scared?"

"No," she replied, her voice shaking. "I don't believe in ghosts, but this story gives me goosebumps."

He leaned in closer. "Believe it or not, Candle Face rewards those who listen to her."

"Candle Face?" My girlfriend and I burst out laughing.

"She hears you," he snapped. "She's everywhere. Always listening."

I couldn't resist another joke. "Does she have a list? Checks it twice?"

Our laughter filled the room, but my friend didn't say another word. He stood up, walked out the door, and disappeared into the night.

"Where's he going?" my girlfriend asked, and I could hear the nerves in her voice.

"I don't know," I said, trying to brush it off. "He gets carried away sometimes. He'll be back. Besides, he lives here."

Fifteen minutes later, he returned, but he wasn't alone. Three men came in with him.

The moment they walked inside, I felt it. One of them carried a machete. Another had a large tarp. Every instinct I had told me to run, and I bolted for the back door. But the rug slipped under my feet, and before I could get back up, they were on me.

"He left you behind," one of them said.

The man with the tarp spread it across the kitchen floor. "Get on the tarp," he said, almost casually. "Makes cleanup easier."

"Do something!" my girlfriend screamed.

I tried to hold my ground. "I'm not getting on that tarp," I said, my voice shaking.

But my friend stepped forward with a cattle prod. He didn't hesitate. He drove it into me, and my body locked up. I hit the floor hard. They dragged me onto the tarp.

The man with the machete didn't waste time. He swung it and cut off my hands one after the other. Another man shoved a gag into my mouth, muffling my screams as they cut me apart. The pain was beyond anything I had known. They kept going until only my torso and head were left whole. I was alive, but barely.

My girlfriend stood frozen, forced to watch while they did it. Then they turned on her and put her through the same thing. They didn't kill her then. Instead, they wrapped both of us in the tarp, loaded us into the trunk of my own car, and drove off.

I remember the ride, every bump, every turn. Our blood pooled under us, soaking into the tarp. We must have driven for about an hour before the car finally stopped.

They dragged us out and dumped us into a dark gravel pit. My body was broken, and my breathing was shallow. My girlfriend lay beside me, barely alive, too.

Some of my blood had spilled onto the floor of the house, but it went unnoticed, hidden from the detectives who questioned my friend soon after the murders. It was as though the evil around that house had swallowed even the evidence.

The last thing I heard was my friend's voice. He sounded detached as he said, "All you had to do was believe."

Now we're trapped in a nightmare. This place is nothing like you could imagine. Shadows move on their own and whisper things you don't want to hear. The air is full of the cries of souls like us, tortured, broken, lost. There's no escape here. No peace.

After the pair vanished as suddenly as they had appeared, I went downstairs to write down their account. This was my third encounter, and by then I had begun to feel a real sense of purpose. I understand now why they're coming to me. I'm here to tell their stories and help free them from Candle Face.

Personal Note to My Readers

These two visitors left behind a violent story. I'm asking for your help in identifying them, finding where their bodies were left, and determining who killed them.

Pay close attention to what they shared. Their final night ended at a childhood friend's house, which became the place where they were attacked. We also know they were driven about an hour in the victim's car, which may help narrow down where their bodies were dumped. Are there gravel pits within an hour of that suspect's home?

Who are these two victims, and where were they taken? We know detectives had already questioned the killer in his own house, but who was he? Any connection, theory, or detail may help this case. Let's work through it together and see where it leads.

A CONVERSATION WITH A CANDLE FACE BELIEVER

November 25, 2023

Tomorrow may turn into an interesting day for an interview. Earlier today, I received an email from someone claiming to have information about Candle Face, the ghost said to haunt the Austin area. He didn't say much, but he seemed eager to talk.

The sender calls himself "Mr. Smoe" and insists that Candle Face helps people find "peace." I'm having trouble making sense of that based on what I've learned so far. How could a ghost that haunts people and is said to kill them be tied to peace? That idea doesn't line up with what the spirits who have contacted me have described. Even so, I'm keeping an open mind. I may not yet understand the full story behind Candle Face.

Mr. Smoe has agreed to let me record our conversation on video, which should help me keep an accurate record of what he says. Once I have the transcript, I'll make it available.

I'm curious. I'm also cautious. We'll see what tomorrow brings.

CANDLE FACE VICTIM #4: THE HOMELESS MAN WITH THE LIMP

November 30, 2023

As I settled into bed tonight, with twilight throwing long shadows across my room, I wasn't surprised to see another spirit appear in the corner, arriving the way the others had before. This one walked toward me with a noticeable limp, and each step carried a clear sense of purpose. I felt an odd calm, probably because I've gotten used to these nightly visits. As he came closer, I could feel that he had come with a story to tell. Then he spoke:

> Every time I limped through downtown Austin, things got quiet. The suit-and-tie types and the folks in fancy clothes would stop talking when I got close, like somebody hit a mute button. As soon as I passed, they'd start right back up, like I

wasn't even there. My limp was steady. Life had hit me hard, and I was still standing. I didn't mind that nobody looked me in the eye. It was better that way. Trusting people was never for me.

Out in the homeless community, we talked a lot about Candle Face. She was a story people held on to, something to pull attention away from the demons in their own heads. Some called her by another name and said she was a savior for broken people. I wanted to believe that too, but no matter how many times I called for her, she never answered. After a while, the silence ate away at what little belief I had left.

When she finally did show up, she came with a scream, raw and piercing. There was nothing gentle in it. Nothing comforting. She ordered me around. She told me I had to serve her and spread her story. Her demands were one more voice in a mind that already had too many. I lashed out, angry and bitter. Whatever faith I had in her was gone by then.

That was my mistake.

One evening, I was sitting on a bench waiting for the bus when the streetlights started to dim. The shadows stretched in ways they shouldn't have. Then she came. Candle Face. Hollow eyes. That gaping, empty mouth. I'll never forget it.

"You do not believe," she hissed. "Your faith is the light that feeds me, and your doubt... your punishment."

Before I could answer, her hot, sizzling hands grabbed my shoulders, and everything went blank. The sounds of the city dropped away as she dragged me into the shadows around that bus stop.

In her lair, she showed me the truth. Candle Face wasn't the savior I had imagined. She ruled over a place where spirits stay trapped by their own skepticism. It was her hell, and then it became mine too.

She gathered the lost, the ones whose belief had run out. She fed on disbelief and turned it into power.

My punishment was becoming part of the haunting. I was one of her stories now.

He nodded as if to thank me, then slowly turned and limped back toward the corner where he had first appeared. Then he faded into nothing. Not wanting to lose any of it, I hurried downstairs and wrote out his story right away.

Personal Note to My Readers

This victim was likely a homeless man who spent a lot of time downtown, though not necessarily someone who slept there every night, since he was waiting for a bus late at night. One strong clue is his noticeable limp.

Has anyone heard of a missing homeless man known for limping and spending time downtown? If so, that may be our lead.

THE CREEK, THE SHADOW, AND CANDLE FACE

December 1, 2023

I recently had a brief interview with someone who says he believes in Candle Face. The interview didn't last long. Things became tense when I asked how he could describe Candle Face as "compassionate" while also saying she harms people who don't believe in her. My questions seemed to irritate Mr. Smoe, and the interview ended earlier than I expected. I did record it, but I promised to let him review it before I shared it anywhere. So far, I haven't heard back from him.

After the interview, I needed to clear my head, so I walked to the creek near my old childhood home. It's a rough area, with steep cliffs and uneven trails, but we loved it as kids. We spent hours there playing games like hide-and-seek and capture the flag. I filmed some of the area and plan to share that footage with the interview, if and when Mr.

Smoe gives his approval.

Later that day, I stopped by a friend's house in Southeast Austin. We ended up talking about the interview and the dreams I have been having, the ones that make me think Candle Face's victims may actually be reaching out to me. While we were talking, something strange happened. His Ring doorbell camera picked up a large dark shadow on the porch and an unusual orb, even though no one was there.

My friend thinks the interview may have stirred something up, especially because both of us grew up knowing how dangerous Candle Face's legend could be.

I'll share the interview, the footage from the creek, and the porch video as soon as I have permission. It has been a strange few days, and I don't get the sense that things are settling down.

AN INTERVIEW WITH A CANDLE FACE BELIEVER

December 3, 2023

Date of interview: 26 Nov 2023

I've spent a lot of time looking into the paranormal, but few stories in Central Texas draw attention like Candle Face. She's said to haunt people who deny her existence, driving them toward a mental breakdown or even death, while her followers claim she can erase pain and mental torment in an instant.

My latest attempt to understand her led me to an interview with a man who calls himself "Mr. Smoe." In some ways, our connection feels personal. He believes I played a role in drawing Candle Face out years ago. During our conversation, he described her one way to believers and another to skeptics. To believers, she's gentle and able to lift unbearable pain. To skeptics, she shows no mercy.

Mr. Smoe's story begins in a troubled home shaped by his father's alcoholism. By thirteen, he says he was already struggling with addiction himself. His life changed in 2002, at a point of complete desperation. Sitting in his living room and ready to commit suicide, he saw a young ghost girl appear. She had hollow eye sockets, skin that bubbled like boiling oil, and a voice that didn't sound human. "Do not do it. I can help you. I can make your pain disappear." Desperate, he answered, "Yes, I believe."

He said the change was immediate. The anguish lifted. The voices in his mind, which had tormented him for years, went silent for the first time. Candle Face retreated into the corner where she had appeared and left him changed.

After that night, she began appearing in his dreams and telling him to spread her presence to others, especially people struggling with addiction. As he spoke at AA meetings, he says he found others who also believed Candle Face had taken away their pain. Over time, his efforts moved beyond meeting halls to people on the streets and those caught in prostitution in South Austin.

There is, however, a darker side to this story. According to Mr. Smoe, people who reject Candle Face don't find relief. They sink further into despair. Some reportedly lose their grip on reality. Others die by suicide.

I pressed Mr. Smoe on that contradiction and asked how she could be both compassionate and cruel. The question seemed to irritate him. He ended the interview abruptly and warned me to watch my step.

Below is the video of our brief interview. Mr. Smoe, clearly a pseudonym, insisted on anonymity. To honor that, I recorded the interview with the camera pointed at his ceiling fan, then edited the footage to brighten it and distort his voice:

www.youtube.com/watch?v=oqmUm8TWJjA

After the interview, I walked to a creek near my childhood home to clear my head. That creek was a well-known shortcut to Dawson Elementary School and a place where neighborhood kids often gathered to play or fight. I filmed the area and thought about how my brother Ricky and I used to move through those trails, and how I once encountered Candle Face there.

www.youtube.com/watch?v=n6Astmk75uA

Later, I visited an old friend who knows Candle Face's legend from our childhood. While we were talking about the interview and the creek, his Ring doorbell camera picked up something unusual. No one was on the porch, but the video showed a large shadow and a strange orb. My friend believes it may have been Candle Face, drawn either by the conversation or by my recent interview.

Note to my friends who know this house and its owner: please keep his identity confidential.

www.youtube.com/watch?v=jubdToQfe8c

I still have trouble making sense of the accounts that describe her as compassionate when so much fear surrounds her. One thing does seem clear. Belief, or the lack of it, plays a major role in how she deals with people. Believers are spared, while those who reject her suffer. But what drives her? Compassion? Vengeance? Something else?

For now, all I can do is document what I find: interviews, visits to places tied to her story, and footage like the Ring camera recording. Whether people believe in Candle Face or not, her effect on those who cross her path is hard to dismiss. She leaves a mark, and I don't think she's finished.

CANDLE FACE VICTIM #5: TOO LATE TO BELIEVE

December 7, 2023

It's been a week since my last nocturnal visitor, and I had started to wonder if they were done coming to me. That's a strange thing to admit. What used to fill me with dread now leaves me waiting for the next encounter, even hoping for it. I've stopped taking afternoon naps, so I'll be tired by nightfall, and instead of staying up late, I'm going to bed early. I want to be ready if another spirit appears.

So far, my role has been simple. I listen to their stories and write them down. I haven't helped them in any real way yet, but I'm still holding on to the hope that one day I may be able to help them find peace.

Then last night, something finally happened. Just after I finished saying my prayers, I noticed movement in the shadows of my room.

At first, it was only a shift in the dark. Then it took shape and became a young woman. She came toward me quickly, as if she had no time to waste, and I could feel how badly she needed to speak. This is what she told me:

It started at a gas station. I was trying to get inside before it got too late, and as I walked in, I noticed a young girl with messy hair pass by me. Something about her pulled at a memory, a story I had heard at the women's group home where I was staying.

Late at night, we would sit around and talk about the ghost of a girl who died in a fire. They said she haunted people who doubted her and punished skeptics. At the time, I barely paid attention. I was too caught up in my own problems, my mental health, and the things I was dealing with every day. The story felt small compared to what was already going on in my life.

That night, standing under the gas station lights, I laughed to myself. "If she were real," I said, "she'd know life has worse demons."

After I left the gas station, I took the longer way back to the group home. I wanted some quiet. I needed time to clear my head. The path ran through a wooded area off the main road. The trees moved in the breeze, and for a moment, it felt calm.

Then I felt it. A sharp heat at the back of my neck, like someone was watching me. I quickened my pace, fighting the urge to look back. Then I heard it. A whisper, so faint I almost missed it. 'Believe...'

My heart started pounding. I turned around, but there was nothing there. Just the woods and the dark. I cursed my imagination and started walking again, faster this time.

Then I saw the glow. It came from the woods to my right, a soft flickering light. I followed it and found an old tent hidden among the trees. The flaps were unzipped, and inside, a single candle was burning. Sitting beside it was a little girl. Her eyes were full of sorrow, and when she looked at me, it felt like she was staring straight through me.

"Do you believe now?" she asked, her voice low.

I froze. "I... I don't know what to believe."

The wind roared without warning and put out the candle. The tent went black, and she was gone.

I ran. Regret hit me with every step. Why had I taken that path? Why had I mocked the story?

A week later, I found myself going back to the gas station. I didn't want to go, but I couldn't leave it alone. I needed to know whether the tent was still there. It was. This time, the flaps were zipped shut. My hands were shaking when I opened them.

Inside, the tent was filled with candles. Their glow lit every corner. And there she was, standing in the center. The flames lit her face.

"Why?" I asked, my voice shaking. "Why me?"

"You needed to believe," she said. "In life, you fought your demons, but you never believed in me. You invalidated my pain, my existence."

Tears ran down my face. "I believe now. I see you. I understand."

The candles flared, their flames reaching toward me. She stepped closer until her face was only inches from mine. "It is too late," she said softly.

Then everything went dark.

Days later, they found my lifeless body in those same woods. The cause of death remained unknown.

The spirit finished her story and looked at me, waiting. For the first time during one of these visits, I sat up in bed. I reached out my hand, and she did the same. Before we could touch, an ear-splitting screech came from the shadowed corner of my room. She pulled back at once, retreated into the portal, and vanished.

I rushed downstairs and wrote down everything I could remember while it was still fresh in my mind.

Personal Note to My Readers

This encounter made me realize how much my reaction to these visits has changed. At first, they terrified me. Now they leave me anxious and focused. I want to understand who these spirits are, what happened to them, and whether there's any way to help them.

The young woman's story felt deeply personal. She was describing her own fear and what it felt like to be ignored until it was too late. When I reached out to her, she felt real to me, someone whose pain had been dismissed and whose belief came too late.

Even the screech from the corner, something that once would have rattled me, only made me more determined to keep going. These spirits are people whose stories didn't end on their own terms. They're demanding to be heard.

CANDLE FACE CHRONICLES: THE LOST SOULS INVESTIGATION

December 11, 2023

As an intelligence analyst and private investigator, I have worked through many difficult cases over the past three decades. Even so, nothing I have dealt with compares to Candle Face. In *Candle Face Chronicles: The Lost Souls*, I'm asking you to work alongside me in an active investigation. These stories are firsthand testimonies from spirits who fell victim to Candle Face, a vengeful ghost who punishes those who deny she exists.

These spirits come to me at night and recount what happened to them. Each one doubted her at some point, only to face her rage directly or through her followers. Their testimonies show how she targets skeptics and punishes them.

I survived my own encounter with Candle Face, and that experience pushed me toward a different purpose. My years in intelligence analysis, missing persons cases, and human trafficking investigations have helped prepare me, but I can't do this alone. I need your help. This is a real investigation, and it's still unfolding.

Here's where you may be able to help:

1. Finding the Lost Souls' remains: Many of these spirits disappeared without a trace, and their bodies were never found. Finding where they were left may help bring them peace. Their accounts sometimes mention places, landmarks, or other details that may point to where their remains are.

2. Identifying their killers: In some cases, Candle Face appears to have told her followers to kill for her. We need to identify who those people were. By studying the spirits' testimonies closely for clues, specific events, locations, or traits, we may be able to work out who was responsible. Once we identify them, law enforcement can take it from there.

Candle Face Chronicles: The Lost Souls asks you to take part in the investigation. You're working with me to locate lost bodies and identify the people who killed them. Their testimonies demand a response. Someone has to decide what to do with them.

You have a role in this investigation. You're helping search for these souls' final resting places and identify their killers. Your research may help their cases and bring some measure of justice to the spirits still suffering in Candle Face's lair.

I'm asking you to stand with me in this project and help those who remain trapped by Candle Face.

Personal Note to My Readers

I'm asking you to take part in something personal and difficult. This book documents disturbing encounters and asks for your help in a real paranormal investigation.

These spirits are victims still asking for help. We need your help finding their remains, identifying their killers, and reaching any living family members. This project is larger than any one person. It depends on careful work and sound judgment.

By working together, we improve our chances of helping these souls and following Candle Face's trail as far as it leads.

Thank you for standing with me in this project. Please visit my website at www.candleface.com to share your findings and join the investigation.

CANDLE FACE VICTIM #6: THE MAN WHO IGNORED THE FLYER

December 13, 2023

My wife and I were getting ready to watch another episode of *Breaking Bad* when I felt an odd nudge, almost like a reminder that I should go to bed earlier than usual, in case another spirit showed up. Then, as if that thought had called him in, a figure stepped out of the portal and walked toward my bed in a sharp business suit. Each step made a clean, measured tap against the floor.

He didn't greet me. He went straight into what he had come to say, and there was no mistaking the urgency in him:

> Surrounded by the noise of the city, I moved through the downtown crowd with tomorrow's numbers already running through my head. The streets were packed with tall buildings, bright

signs, and the kind of noise that never really stops. Beggars sat in doorways. Cafes were full. Somewhere off in the distance, there was live music.

My own life felt far removed from all of it. It was meetings, calls, quarterly targets, and one deadline after another. In the corporate world, people knew me for getting results. Boardrooms were where I made my living, and my mind was the only thing I fully trusted. I did well in that world, and I told myself that was enough. I didn't spend much time thinking about what I had pushed aside to keep it going. Calls I let go to voicemail. Birthdays I missed. Nights in an apartment that was too clean because nobody was ever in it. When those thoughts came up, I buried them under work.

As I walked through the crowd, caught up in my own thoughts, I noticed someone watching me.

He stood at the corner of Congress Avenue and Sixth Street, a ragged man holding out a worn flyer. His clothes were old, and his hands shook, but it was his eyes that drew my attention. They looked desperate.

"Excuse me, sir," he said, holding the flyer out to me. "Please, take a moment to read this. It's about our mother. She has saved countless lives. You could be next."

I barely looked at it. I took the paper, crushed it in my hand, and let it fall.

"Not interested," I said.

I kept walking, already back to thinking about a morning meeting, a client call, and what the market might do before noon.

But that night, back in my apartment, I kept seeing that man's eyes and hearing his voice. My apartment, expensive and spotless, felt warmer than usual. It felt tight, like the walls were pressing in. For the first time, I saw it clearly. Clean counters. No dishes in the sink. No sound except the vent. No one there but me.

I told myself it was nothing. Stress, maybe. A long day. But as I lay in bed staring at the ceiling, I heard a female voice this time. It was faint, like something trying to get through the noise in my head.

Then the light flickered.

When I turned, she was there.

Candle Face.

Her presence is hard to describe. She was horrifying, and there was something about her I still can't explain. She looked as if she were made of shadow and light, her body flickering like a candle flame.

"Do you still disbelieve, businessman?" she asked, her voice low and calm.

I couldn't move. When I tried to speak, the words came out broken. "This... this can't be real. You're... you're not real."

Her laughter held no warmth. "You laughed at my warning," she said. "You brushed aside the man I sent to you. That brought me here."

She reached toward me, her hand more shadow than flesh, and I felt the heat from it before it touched me. I was so scared, I thought I might black out. All the things I trusted, logic, routine, control, meant nothing with her standing over me.

When her fingers touched my forehead, it felt as though something had split open inside me. My whole life moved in front of me. Not the big moments. The smaller ones. Calls I let ring out. Dinners I canceled. Faces I hadn't thought about in years came back to me. Family. Friends. People I had pushed aside. They looked tired of waiting on me.

Too late, I understood what I'd traded away. Again and again, I had chosen work first and told myself everything else could wait.

I begged her for mercy. I told her I could change, that I wanted to believe. It made no difference.

"It is too late," she said.

She took my soul and pulled me into her lair.

The next day, the city kept moving. People at work would have noticed I was gone, but the streets didn't. My apartment stayed exactly as I had left it, clean, quiet, and empty.

And somewhere on those same streets, the ragged man stood at another corner, holding out his flyer. His eyes searched the crowd, pleading for someone to stop and listen.

After the businessman finished his testimony, he stepped backward into the portal in the corner of my bedroom, his shoes tapping just as they had when he entered. Before he disappeared, he said one more thing:

Slow down long enough to listen to the people around you. Don't wait until it's too late to see what really matters.

Personal Note to My Readers

The businessman's testimony makes one thing clear: we often fail to listen, both to the living and to those who feel ignored. In the rush of daily life, it's easy to brush past someone's warning, pain, or plea, the same way he dismissed that flyer. A friend's concern, a stranger's request, a loved one's silence, any of those can hold something we miss when we're moving too fast.

His final words carried a warning and an attempt to offer something back. He was telling us to slow down and pay attention to what people around us are saying. We already have chances every day to listen better without something supernatural forcing us to see it.

CANDLE FACE VICTIM #7: SHE BELIEVED, BUT WOULD NOT OBEY

December 15, 2023

I stayed up later than usual tonight, figuring there wouldn't be a visit since these encounters usually happen every five to eight days. My wife had gone to bed earlier, so I was by myself, scrolling through Facebook and watching YouTube videos.

That's when it happened. I caught movement out of the corner of my eye coming from the sunroom, which was completely dark by midnight.

She was there, hovering as if she were waiting for me to notice her. I opened the double doors and stepped into the room. I must have gotten too close because she backed away a few steps. She looked tired. She looked worn down, but I could also see how badly she needed to tell me something.

Once she started speaking, she had to keep stopping, her words breaking under deep sobs. Even so, she kept trying to steady herself and tell me what happened:

It started in the fall of 2011. That was when everything changed for me. At first, it seemed simple enough. I'd be in my bedroom, late at night, with the room cold and quiet. Then I'd see something moving in the corner. It was Candle Face.

She would come to the foot of my bed and kneel there in front of me. She wouldn't move for a while. She wouldn't say anything. She would just stay there and look at me. Then, when she finally spoke, her voice was low. "Do you believe?"

I did believe. I always had, even when people around me laughed it off or treated it like some local story. So I told her yes. My heart was pounding so hard it hurt. I was terrified. Even so, I felt drawn in.

She said, "Thank you."

Then it would end, and I would wake up gasping in the early morning light, trying to tell myself it was only a dream.

But after a while, it stopped feeling like a dream. She started taking me to places I can't describe, wide empty places where she showed me what she did to people who didn't believe in her. I could hear them screaming. Every time, she

would look at me and say, "Bring more to me."
Then I would wake up soaked in sweat.

Then one night, I was lying in bed watching TV
when the room changed. The shadows stretched
across the walls, and she came out of the corner
again. This time, she looked more solid. More
real.

"Find them," she said angrily. "Bring me the
disbelievers, and I'll reward you."

I was shaking, but I answered her. I said, "I
believe in you. I still won't do this. I won't bring
them to you."

She came closer.

"Belief is only the beginning," she said. "Your soul
is the prize."

Then she said it again. "Bring me the disbelievers,
and I'll reward you."

It kept happening after that. Over and over. I
could still hear her voice during the day, even
when she wasn't there. But I wouldn't do what
she wanted. I wouldn't help her.

Then one night, she came back angrier than ever.
I knew right away something was different. I
couldn't move. She started at my feet and began
taking me piece by piece. I don't know how else
to say it. The pain was worse than anything I had
ever felt. It burned through me until there was
nothing left.

> Now I'm not fully myself anymore. Part of me is
> with her. I see what she sees. I watch her move
> through the night. I watch her go after people
> who deny her. I'm still there, but I can't stop any
> of it. I can't get away.

She retreated into the corner where she had appeared. Before disappearing completely, she said, "Help me, Ray. Please find my body somewhere in the Barton Creek Greenbelt..."

Before she could say anything else, two smoking arms burst from the portal behind her. With such force that her legs lifted off the ground, she was yanked back into it. The scream that came with it was filled with agony and fear, and it seemed to echo through the whole house.

I hurried downstairs, needing to write down every detail she had shared. My hands were shaking, and I felt sick with guilt over what had just happened to her, maybe because she had told me too much. In the rush, I lost some of the finer details of her story, and I'm sorry for that.

Personal Note to My Readers

This is the second time I've seen a spirit suffer for either reaching out to me or saying too much. I've been doing my best to help these Lost Souls, and now I'm starting to worry that I haven't held up my end of this. As I keep sharing their stories, it's getting harder to ignore the possibility that I may be making things worse.

The doubts are getting stronger. I keep asking myself whether I'm the right person for this. So far, I haven't been able to help them in any real way.

I don't think I can keep doing this alone. If any paranormal investigators, mediums, or psychics are willing to get involved, I could use your help.

CANDLE FACE VICTIM #8: A PARANORMAL INVESTIGATOR'S ENCOUNTER WITH CANDLE FACE

December 21, 2023

I've realized I can't handle these Lost Souls on my own, so I've been actively searching for paranormal investigators, mediums, and psychics across different online platforms. I have posted on Facebook, Reddit, and even the Darknet, a space I became familiar with during my years investigating missing persons and human trafficking cases. I'm trying to find someone who can make sense of the messages from my nocturnal visitors.

Unfortunately, most of what I find leads to groups focused on minor things like orbs, which are often just dust, and blurry ghost photos that are usually pareidolia. They tend to avoid serious hauntings or real cases, and that has been discouraging. Every dead end leaves me feeling more responsible for these spirits, and I worry that I'm failing them.

I finally got a call from a group of paranormal investigators who were interested in my nightly visitations. During a three-way video call, I explained Candle Face's background and the visions that have been haunting me. They recommended a full investigation of my old Austin neighborhood and the creek where Candle Face has reportedly been seen. We're planning to do that sometime in mid to late January. Part of me wants to see what we might learn. Another part of me is scared about what we might find.

That same night, I slept in the living room instead of my usual place in the upstairs guest bedroom. My wife, still recovering from multiple surgeries, was sleeping alone for comfort, and my son, who was home for Christmas, was using the guest room where the Lost Souls usually appear. I left the kitchen light on, which cast a faint shadow in the far corner of the living room, in case another spirit showed up.

As I started drifting off, one of those shadows shifted along the wall until it took the form of a woman in her thirties, around five feet eight.

She walked toward the couch with a kind of calm that was hard to place. "It's my turn," she said quietly, as if the moment had been waiting for her. She told me her visit had been prompted by the call I had with the paranormal team earlier that day. She said she had been a paranormal investigator in the mid-2000s and had once investigated Candle Face herself. She begged me not to involve this new team, especially if they planned to treat it lightly. She warned that there was real danger, especially for the male investigator who liked to use humor in his investigations. Before she began, she asked that her family be left in peace and urged others not to dig too deeply into Candle Face's history.

This is her story:

As a paranormal investigator, I approached legends and ghost stories with skepticism. When I heard about Candle Face, I assumed it was another urban myth. I came to Austin determined to disprove it.

Over several nights, I tried everything: séances, equipment, and visits to places like Ben Howell Drive, the nearby creek, and Lady Bird Lake, where some people claimed Candle Face had drowned her victims. But nothing happened. No strange activity. No flickering lights. Not even a cold breeze. I became convinced the whole story was folklore.

Because of that, I wrote a blog post saying Candle Face was a hoax. I mocked the legend and called it one of Austin's more imaginative ghost stories, but nothing more than that. I went to bed that night satisfied and ready for the next case.

That same night, the shadows in my hotel room began to move. At first, I thought exhaustion was playing tricks on me. Then she appeared. Candle Face. Her charred figure was worse than anything I had read. She mocked me for not believing and for the fear I couldn't hide. Her laugh wasn't human. Then she was gone, leaving me frozen in place and questioning everything.

The next day, I thought about changing my article to reflect what I had seen, but my pride got in the way. I told myself that what was done was done.

Back home in San Antonio, she came to me again, this time in my bedroom. She was furious. She demanded that I rewrite the article, acknowledge her, and spread her story. When I refused, she made a promise of her own. She said she would create a story about me and send it out to her believers.

She began to speak, laying out my fate as if it had already happened:

The Hunter Becomes the Haunted

Behold the tale of the skeptic who dared to doubt me. You sought to expose me, to solve a case you deemed false. But now, the hunter becomes the haunted.

You thought you were brave, seeking out spirits. Yet, when faced with me, your courage crumbled like ash. Watching you paralyzed with fear was amusing, contradicting your bold claims.

I have decided your fate, dear paranormal investigator. Since you refused to correct your story, I shall create my own about you. Your story will be eternally haunting, and my image and laughter will constantly be in your mind.

Each night, as you try to sleep, you will hear my voice and see my charred face. You will long for peace, but it will elude you, just as the truth did.

And when the burden becomes too much, you will reach for pills to still your heart; remember, it was your disbelief that sealed your fate. You will be a warning to all who dare to investigate me.

You wanted to find the truth, and now you live it. You are mine now, dear paranormal investigator. Your story ends with me.

I lived in constant fear, haunted by Candle Face and tormented by her laughter. I wish I had rewritten that article. I deleted my website and destroyed my equipment, thinking I could escape her, but the suffering followed me. It never stopped.

After a year of living with her haunting me, I reached for a bottle of pills. Even in death, I have found no peace. I'm trapped now with the others who doubted her. Remorse consumes me because I dismissed something that was real.

After she finished, she stepped backward into the corner of my living room. One last time, she begged me to call off the paranormal investigation in January or at least make sure the team approached it with caution, not humor.

Personal Note to My Readers

My encounter with this former paranormal investigator, who somehow knew about my conversation with a ghost-hunting team just hours earlier, has given me a new idea. If spirits really can sense us during the day, then maybe that awareness can be used to help them. It seems what we do in the living world can affect them, and their presence can affect us in return.

I'm now thinking about speaking to these spirits more directly during the day. I plan to mention their stories out loud and try to address their issues whenever I can. Maybe by giving them direct attention and actively looking for answers, I can help give them some relief.

This has changed the way I think about the paranormal. It feels immediate now, almost reactive. If that's true, then paying attention to these spirits and responding to them may be one of the few ways to help them.

CANDLE FACE VICTIM #9: SACRIFICED BY HER FRIENDS

December 27, 2023

I've been spending my nights in the living room again, leaving the kitchen light on. The glow casts just enough of a silhouette in the far corner for any nocturnal visitors to step forward. As I fought off sleep tonight, I saw the shadows start to move, a clear sign that someone, or something, had arrived.

Out of the portal stepped a young woman who looked young enough to still be in high school. This time, I tried something different. I sat up and waved her over, inviting her to sit beside me. She glanced back at the dark corner and looked uncertain. Then she stayed where she was and went straight into her story. Her words came fast and tight, and I found myself worrying that her raised voice might wake everyone in the house, or even the neighbors.

This is her story:

High school graduation was coming up, and my friends and I decided to have one last slumber party. It was at my best friend's house, an old place that always felt dusty and worn out. We stayed up late talking about crushes, our plans, and what came next, even though I think all of us were nervous about it. Then the conversation shifted. My best friend brought up the ghost everybody in South Austin seemed to know about.

"Do you believe in Candle Face?" she asked.

I laughed. "Of course not."

The other girls gasped. They looked at me like I had said something I shouldn't have.

"You have to believe," they told me. "She goes after people who don't."

I brushed it off. "I just don't believe," I said.

My best friend leaned forward, calm as ever. "Then let's summon her," she said. "Let her see for herself. Maybe she'll spare you."

That night, my friends gathered around a flickering candle. They chanted strange words in low voices. I stood off to the side, watching them with amusement and disbelief. It all felt ridiculous to me.

When nothing happened, I laughed again. "Where's your Candle Face now?" I said, louder than I meant to.

A few days later, I disappeared. The same friends who had stood in that room with me joined the search parties and called my name, but they were never going to find me. My body was underwater. With my last breaths, Candle Face told me what had happened.

"Your friends sacrificed you to me," she said. "They did it to protect themselves."

That betrayal hurt more than death itself. I said, "Grant me my last wish. I want them to live with guilt and suffer for it."

Candle Face tilted her head and smiled. "I like the way you think," she said.

After that, my wish became their curse. Over the years, I watched guilt wear them down. Their lives fell apart under the weight of what they had done.

Trying to escape it, they gathered years later in that same house and summoned my spirit, begging me to forgive them. I said nothing. Candle Face appeared instead.

"You betrayed your friend," she told them. "For that, you are bound to her curse. You will suffer until death finally takes you."

My best friend pleaded, "We believe in you. Please, let us go."

Candle Face's face hardened. "Yes, you believe," she said. "But you did not betray your friend for me. You did it for yourselves. You sacrificed her to save your own lives. There is no mercy for that."

That's where they're now. Trapped in torment, with no one coming to save them.

Personal Note to My Readers

During her visit, the spirit showed almost no fear. Anger drove her to tell what happened. Her resentment toward the friends who betrayed her was plain. Candle Face seemed to respect her final wish and fully embraced the curse she placed on them.

I get the sense that this spirit feels more at ease in Candle Face's lair than she ever did in life. Her tie to Candle Face seems strong, as if their shared betrayal bound them together in ways I don't fully understand yet.

THE EMPTY LOT NEXT DOOR: THE ORIGIN OF CANDLE FACE

December 28, 2023

Let me share the story I wrote about in my memoir, *The Empty Lot Next Door*. It began in the 1970s, when my family moved from the city projects to a small house in Austin, Texas. Back then, I was just a kid called Ray, and I was immediately drawn to the empty lot next door, a strange place where a house once stood, leaving behind nothing but a gaping hole in the back.

Our new neighborhood was packed with kids, and we turned that lot into our own playground. But it wasn't just an ordinary patch of dirt. The lot came with a grim tale that both intrigued and terrified me. The house that once stood there had burned down years earlier, and rumor had it that a little girl died in the fire. According to the local kids, her ghost still haunted the lot, targeting anyone daring or foolish enough to jump into that hole.

Being young and reckless, I couldn't resist the challenge. I decided to test the ghost story, and it's a decision I've regretted ever since. That's when I first encountered the ghost I came to call "Candle Face," named for her charred appearance. She invaded my dreams and even left handprints around the house in broad daylight.

But the story behind *The Empty Lot Next Door* goes deeper than a ghost. It came out of survival, kids left to fend for themselves while their parents worked long hours, and the despair and helplessness that came with facing real and imagined horrors. Sibling abuse, bullying, and trauma left marks that shaped all of us in ways we didn't fully understand at the time.

One day, armed with newfound courage, I faced Candle Face in a standoff I can only describe as fierce and terrifying. In the end, I thought I had defeated her, banishing her back to hell. Or so I believed.

After high school, I enlisted in the Army. My time there allowed me to see the world and sharpen my analytical and investigative skills. In 2010, I wrote *The Empty Lot Next Door*, hoping it would bring closure for me, my family, and the friends who had been touched by those events. For a time, it did. But closure can be fleeting.

Now that I'm retired and back in Texas, I've revisited my past with fresh eyes. After more than three decades as an intelligence analyst and investigator, I've decided to find out whether Candle Face was real or just a product of childhood trauma. If she's real, is she still out there? And who was she before she died?

Over the years, I've received countless emails from people claiming to have encountered Candle Face. I used to brush them off. But being back here made me curious enough to follow up. Most of the people I contacted were too terrified to talk, fearing her revenge.

One man, an 82-year-old named Mr. John Doe, stood out. Unlike the others, he seemed eager to share his experiences.

I met with him in October 2023 under strict conditions of anonymity. During our face-to-face interview, Mr. Doe shared his account of the fire that destroyed the house next to where I grew up. According to him, the fire started when the father spilled gasoline while cleaning a car carburetor in the kitchen. Tragically, a young boy named Paul died in that fire. His body was later recovered from the wreckage.

This clashed with what my friends and I had always believed as kids. We thought it was a young girl who had died and become Candle Face.

More than his account of the fire, I kept thinking about Mr. Doe's belief in Candle Face. He described an encounter near the creek at Wilson and El Paso Streets in 1990 and offered me a piece of advice: 'It's better to believe, just in case. It's akin to an insurance policy. If you believe, you're safe. If not, you might end up with a visit.'

Since that interview, my nights have turned into a blur of nightmares much like the ones Mr. Doe described. Candle Face seems to be part of them, but the voices are harder to place. Some rise in shouts. Others fade into whispers. I can't make out what they're saying, but the experience is frightening. I'm surrounded by voices that argue, cry, and plead.

Are these visions hallucinations, or are they messages from Candle Face herself? Whatever the case, her story isn't over.

Maybe she's been waiting for me all along. Now I'm searching for answers, hoping that understanding this nightmare might help me bring it under control or finally bring it to an end.

CANDLE FACE VICTIM #10: THE DEVIL'S MARK

December 30, 2023

Last night, I slept on the couch again. As usual, I left a light on so it would cast that familiar shadow in the far corner for my nighttime visitors. This time, a spirit appeared just as I was drifting off. She carried more anger than sadness. She looked around my living room as if she expected someone else to be there. When she saw I was alone, she came closer but stayed in the shadows, keeping enough distance to hide her face.

This is her story:

> Our group always met at this old café. We'd sit there for hours talking about whatever came up. That night, somebody brought up Candle Face.

My friends talked about her like she was real, like she was some vengeful ghost. I didn't believe any of it. To show how little I cared, I showed them my devil tattoo. It's on my butt. It was stupid, just me trying to be funny and prove I wasn't scared. They laughed, and I laughed too. At the time, it didn't seem like a big deal.

But after that, Candle Face stopped feeling like some made-up story. She started showing up in my dreams. At first, it was just faint voices and hissing, like she was somewhere close but not close enough to see. Then she started talking to me directly. She told me to kill for her and go after people who didn't believe. I said no every time. She almost seemed to enjoy that.

My friends started noticing something was wrong with me. They said I seemed off. Distracted. Distant. They told me I should talk to somebody. They sounded concerned, or at least I thought they did. I never told them about the dreams. I didn't want to scare them, and I didn't want to admit how scared I was.

Then the dreams got worse. One night, Candle Face pulled me from my bed into the shadows. The air was hot, and it was hard to move, like I was trying to push through water. I could see faces in the dark. My friends' faces. I couldn't see them clearly, but I could hear them talking. Whatever they were saying seemed to make her stronger. That was when I realized they were part of it.

The next day, I went to the café like I always did, but I looked at them differently. I listened more closely. They knew too much. The way they talked about Candle Face felt too easy, too specific. That was when I understood I was already part of it.

That night, Candle Face came for me again. She was clearer than ever.

"Are you ready to meet the devil?" she asked.

I laughed in her face. "The friends who sold me out scare me more than the devil ever could," I said.

I was still laughing when the shadows closed around me and she took me into her lair.

The next day, my seat at the café was empty. My friends pretended to mourn, but they knew what had happened. They had a hand in it, and they knew it.

After she finished, she gave me a strained smile and let out a nervous laugh before slipping back into the portal. Once she was gone, I sat there replaying her words. Her story was full of betrayal, and it left me wondering how much fear can override loyalty. Candle Face herself has mentioned betrayal more than once. I still have a lot to figure out.

Personal Note to My Readers

During this encounter, I tried harder than usual to follow her words and get a better look at her. I wanted to see her features more clearly and understand her story with more precision. But she seemed to pick up on the extra attention and kept moving deeper into the shadows, staying out of sight.

That made one thing clear. She noticed the change in how I was dealing with her, and I think it cut the encounter short. Going forward, I need to be more careful in how I approach these spirits. They are sharing painful and deeply personal experiences, and I don't want to push them away.

Handling these encounters by myself isn't easy, but each one is teaching me something. I only hope I'm learning fast enough to help them.

MY NOCTURNAL VISITORS: ALLIES OR ADVERSARIES?

January 2, 2024

Over the last eleven weeks, my sleep has taken me somewhere I didn't expect. What began as occasional dreams once a week, filled with strange images and coded messages, has grown into something larger. At first, the dreams felt disconnected, as if they came from a place I couldn't make sense of. I dreaded going to bed because I knew I would be pulled back into those episodes.

But recently, something changed. It feels as though a barrier has lifted, and I can now understand each dream more clearly. I wake up every morning with the need to write down every detail, every feeling, and every word before it fades. My unease has given way to a sense of purpose. I no longer think these dreams are random flashes in my mind. They seem to open a view into a hidden world of spirits, each one trying to be heard. The shadowy figures I first saw have become distinct voices, each with its own fear, hope, and account.

It's strange that these spirits chose me as the one to speak for them, especially since I'm the person who uncovered and supposedly defeated Candle Face. Her name has spread among these restless souls. They seem to see me as someone who faced her and survived, which gives them reason to hope. Now they're trusting me to tell their stories, find their remains, and identify their killers. But why would Candle Face allow them to reach me? Could this be another trap? Could she be using them to study my habits and weaknesses?

I also keep wondering what these encounters really are, if they're dreams at all. Are they testing my resolve or my judgment? Could something I do give Candle Face more power? I can't ignore the possibility that others, both living and dead, also have a stake in this. Are these spirits truly asking for help, or are some of them leading me in the wrong direction? The uncertainty forces me to question everything, including whether Candle Face, or even some of the spirits themselves, may be trying to manipulate me.

Even with all of that, I'm committed to giving these spirits a voice. I'm bringing their accounts to the page through my journal and other writing, and in doing so, I have become the one left to speak for them. But this role is starting to break me down. I have looked for help from paranormal investigators, mediums, and psychics, but so far, no one has stepped up. The only exception has been a team that mixes comedy with ghost hunting, and that isn't what these spirits need. These spirits need help, not a comedy show.

So each night, sleep has become a mix of anticipation and caution. I want to hear what these spirits have to say, and I stay on guard because of Candle Face. She and I have history, and I suspect these visits are part of something larger she's doing. When I lie down, I try to stay open to the spirits while also preparing myself for whatever Candle Face may be setting in motion.

It's not easy to balance empathy with self-protection. Part of me wants to be fully present and take in everything these spirits share. But I also have to stay alert for signs that Candle Face is behind something. Every dream and every clue has to be dealt with carefully. Understanding how she operates gives me a better chance of protecting both myself and the spirits depending on me.

This has become the center of my life. It's unpredictable and risky, but the chance to help these spirits find some kind of closure, and maybe keep Candle Face in check, is worth it. I intend to keep going, no matter how complicated it gets.

Personal Note to My Readers

I want to invite you into what has been happening since these dream encounters began eleven weeks ago. The fear I felt at first has faded. These encounters feel like contact from a world filled with spirits, each carrying its own story. These spirits have pulled me out of the role of bystander. I'm now speaking for them as best I can.

There's another side to this as well. I'm also the same person who once stood against Candle Face. That history may be part of why these spirits came to me, but it may also be why Candle Face remains on the edge of all this. Each night, I go to sleep knowing I may have to do both jobs at once: listen to the spirits and remain watchful for her.

I'm writing these accounts to bring their stories into the open while also trying to understand Candle Face's purpose. I hope you'll keep following this work as I continue sorting through what the spirits are saying and what Candle Face may be trying to do.

If you want to take part in this effort, please visit my website: www.candleface.com.

CANDLE FACE: THE GHOST NO ONE DARES TO FACE

January 5, 2024

Please allow me to rant.

It's been grueling since I reopened my investigation into Candle Face in October 2023, the ghost that haunted my childhood in Austin, Texas. I had believed I banished her back to hell. My return to Texas after retiring from the military forced me to face something worse. Candle Face was still active, and she was still terrorizing people. With three decades of experience in intelligence analysis and investigations behind me, I set out to understand how far her power had spread.

As I went through the stack of emails I had received over the years about Candle Face, my skepticism turned to alarm. She seemed more powerful than before and more dangerous than ever. Emails from so-called disciples of Candle Face described a spirit that rewarded followers and viciously punished skeptics. For all the fear in their stories, though, most of these people said very little that I could use. Their fear kept them from saying much of value.

My investigation led me into paranormal groups on Facebook, Reddit, and the Darknet, where I found paranormal hobbyists, ghost hunters, mediums, and psychics. That only made my frustration worse.

Many people posting images of "orbs" on these platforms seem fully convinced that their photos show real paranormal activity. Alongside those are the usual cloud photos and grainy pictures of patterns on walls, ceilings, trees, bushes, and other surfaces, most of which are classic examples of pareidolia, people seeing meaningful images in random or unclear visual patterns. The problem is that once these claims are challenged, the reaction often turns personal. Some posters take any skepticism as an attack and quickly accuse others of bullying. To be fair, some skeptics are rude about it. Others are more measured. Even so, the pattern is hard to miss. The paranormal community is often caught in a constant fight between belief and skepticism, and that fight gets worse when people are deeply invested in what they think they have seen.

When I tried to draw these groups into a serious discussion about Candle Face, most of the responses were evasive or openly fearful. Most of these people don't seem interested in real hauntings. They seem more comfortable staying with safer topics like orbs and pareidolia. That tells me a lot. For all their talk about the paranormal, many of them avoid anything that feels truly dangerous. Their interest seems limited to the harmless end of the subject. It doesn't seem to extend to the kind of case I was dealing with.

Watching paranormal investigators was even more frustrating. Many of them post videos of their ghost hunts. These so-called professionals yell at spirits, provoke them, and act brave for the camera, then panic and run the moment something happens that they can't explain. Their behavior comes off as hypocritical. They claim to want real paranormal evidence, yet bolt the second they think they might have found it. Even the ones who stay to the end tend to leave right as the video cuts off, often at the exact sixty-minute mark, which just happens to match the runtime of all their other videos.

My attempts to get help from mediums and psychics went no better. These are people who claim to have direct contact with the spirit world, yet many of them went quiet or turned evasive when I asked for help interpreting the dreams involving Candle Face's victims. That kind of hesitation is hard to ignore. They speak openly about spirits until the case in front of them feels dangerous. Then they back away.

There was one possible lead. I received an offer from a paranormal investigation team during a Facebook video call. They volunteered to investigate Candle Face, the ghost that terrorized my childhood and now seems to be resurfacing. At first, that sounded promising. After looking into them, I lost confidence in what they could offer. Their methods felt more like a comedy routine than a serious investigation. Candle Face's victims need answers, not a late-night performance.

This investigation into Candle Face has been frustrating. I have had to work through skepticism, fear, and too many half-serious efforts from people who claim they want the truth. I have run into more obstacles than answers. The paranormal community may be full of enthusiasm and stories, but much of it backs away when a case becomes truly disturbing. Even so, I'm not backing off. For the people still being haunted by Candle Face, and for what happened to me as a child, this investigation isn't over.

CANDLE FACE VICTIM #11: THE GIRL FROM THE SHACK

January 11, 2024

Last night, as I settled in to sleep on the couch, the eleventh ghostly visitor entered my living room. Her account was the most sorrowful and horrifying one I have heard so far. She began her testimony through sobs of agony. For the first time, I felt the same torment one of these visitors had endured. It's something I hope I never experience again. This is her testimony:

> I had always been shaped by skepticism. My parents, both rationalists to the core, taught me to question everything and look for logical explanations. So that was how I moved through life. I questioned, I analyzed, and I doubted. It was second nature to me.

Then I met him.

My boyfriend of two years saw the world very differently. He was a dreamer who believed in mystery, magic, and the supernatural without embarrassment.

One night, we were sitting together in his dim living room, planning to watch a string of horror movies. The idea was simple. We wanted to scare ourselves. But as the night went on, the distance between the way we saw the world became harder to ignore.

"Do you believe in ghosts?" he asked, his eyes catching the light from the television.

I laughed. My disbelief was firm. "Of course not," I said. "Ghosts are nothing more than figments of our imagination."

He leaned in, speaking low, almost as if he were letting me in on something. "But think about it. Cultures all over the world believe in ghosts, in spirits that remain after death. They can't all be wrong."

I brushed that aside. "Superstition and folklore," I said. "Stories people make up to explain what they don't understand. Nothing more."

That night, he told me a story he had heard from a friend. It was about a cruel spirit, a young female ghost called Candle Face. According to the story, she tormented people who refused to believe in her, driving some of them into madness. Others she killed.

I answered with a dismissive laugh and a shake of my head. To me, ghost stories were for gullible people. I couldn't understand how anyone could truly fear something like that.

It wasn't long before I started having vivid dreams about Candle Face.

In the first one, she looked harmless, almost sweet. She sat across from me at a quiet playground, her small fingers pushing grains of sand around. Her face stayed hidden in shadow as she asked, "Do you believe in me?"

Without hesitation, I said, "No." It was only a dream, I told myself. Maybe a leftover effect from the movies we had watched. Maybe the drugs in my system.

But as the nights passed, Candle Face kept returning, and each time she became worse. In one dream, she sat on my chest, her ghostly fingers tightening around my throat. I woke up gasping.

Then came the dream that left marks on my body. Candle Face lay on top of me, her lips pressed against my neck, leaving grotesque hickeys behind. In what sounded like pleasure, she whispered into my ear, "You're going to be famous with the demons in hell."

I woke in a cold sweat, my neck covered in painful marks. My throat felt tight from the sensation that something had been wrapped around it. I touched the red welts circling my neck. I couldn't tell anyone where they came from, not even my best friends. They all blamed my boyfriend and assumed he had done it.

One evening in the July heat, my boyfriend and I made a reckless choice to get away from our families and their judgment. Our relationship had always caused tension. I was barely eighteen, and he was well into his late twenties. He also kept company with a group of men who were often too much, even on a good day.

That night, we were in a hotel room when his phone rang. He stepped outside to take the call, and even though he tried to sound casual, there was strain in his voice. When he came back in, I could see tension in his face.

"Some friends are coming over," he said.

A few minutes later, three men walked into the room. The whole atmosphere changed. I wanted to get out of there, but it became clear very quickly that they had no intention of letting me leave.

As I started gathering my things, the room blurred. I felt the sting of a needle, and then a heavy paralysis began working through my body. They had drugged me. As they carried me out of the room, everything went black.

The shack they took me to was isolated and miserable, miles outside Austin. A single weak bulb hung from the ceiling and threw shifting shadows across the walls. As my vision cleared, I understood what had been done to me. I was naked, tied to a narrow bed, and there were four chairs lined up against the wall.

For the next six days, men came in one after another and raped me repeatedly. Each chair held a man waiting his turn. There were probably more outside. With every thrust, every minute of pain, I felt another part of myself being stripped away.

But it didn't stop there. On the sixth day, another presence entered the room, one the men didn't seem to notice. It was Candle Face. She moved through the room with a calm that made her even worse. She sang lullabies. She stroked my hair like she was comforting me while the men lay on top of me. Sometimes her fingers burned into my skin and left fresh marks behind.

"Why?" I managed to ask her while one of the men was having his way with me.

"Because," she said with a twisted smile, "my existence becomes more real with every scar, every burn, and, in your case, every stroke."

By the end of the sixth night, the men were gone. I was alone in that shack with Candle Face. She continued where they had left off and kept me in torment through the rest of the night.

At first light, the shack door opened again. The three men came back with my boyfriend. When he looked at me, his eyes were full of tears and betrayal.

"You have to finish it," one of the men said, shoving him forward.

My boyfriend came toward me with a knife shaking in his hand. We locked eyes. In that moment, I saw exactly what he had done to me. He leaned in and whispered, "I'm sorry," then drove the knife into my heart.

As my life left me, Candle Face stood over me. "Thank you," she said, her fingers moving through my hair one last time. "You have made me real."

My sight dimmed. But even in death, one thought came over me as I lay in a shallow grave to the right of the shack. We fear what we don't understand. But sometimes the real monsters stand beside us, and we help create them through our disbelief.

I could tell she had more to say, but what followed was swallowed by the worst sobbing I have ever heard. She gave a faint apology before stepping back into the portal. As she left, it looked as though blood had been smeared across my floor. I turned on the lights and looked for it, expecting to find it there. There was nothing. But the sharp metallic smell of fresh blood still hung in the air.

Personal Note to My Readers

Her story contains clues that may point to her remains and to the people responsible for killing her.

Her testimony calls for an active investigation. She's asking for what should have been hers all along: the chance for justice, and the chance for her life to be brought to a proper end.

So I'm asking you to read her testimony carefully. Look for the clues in her words. Piece together what you can about where she was taken, where she was buried, and who killed her. If enough of us work through it seriously, we may be able to solve this case.

I want to solve her case. Your research may help a spirit still trapped in the pain of what was done to her.

Join me on my website and take part in the investigation: www.candleface.com.

CANDLE FACE VICTIM #12: LAUGHING AT THE WATER'S EDGE

January 23, 2024

It had been two weeks since my last nocturnal visitor. I was starting to think they had all given up on me, assuming I couldn't help them. I've tried, though. I've reached out to a long list of supposed paranormal "experts," from investigators to mediums and psychics, and I have even shared the spirits' testimonies on a podcast. So far, no one has stepped forward in any serious way.

Then last night, while I was in the kitchen making a snack, I heard the sunroom door creak open. My first thought was that someone had broken in, and I braced myself. But when I turned, I found another Lost Soul, another victim of Candle Face.

He was a middle-aged man, soaked from head to toe, and he stayed mostly in the shadows as he came toward me. For some reason,

I felt relief. After two weeks of silence, seeing him reassured me that I hadn't been abandoned. Without any prompting, he began telling me what happened.

It was a warm night, and I was stumbling home from a party. My steps were unsteady, and I was still laughing at the ghost stories we'd been joking about all evening. The one about a young ghost girl? Ridiculous.

I was too busy amusing myself to notice the streetlights dimming one by one.

"Believe in some kid ghost?" I scoffed into the night, louder than I meant to. "It's all just a bunch of BS."

Then she appeared. She stepped out from the treeline on the north side of Longhorn Dam so suddenly it felt like she'd been standing there the whole time, waiting for me to say it.

"You do not believe," she said, her voice calm.

I tried to laugh it off, but my voice shook. "This can't be real," I said, and I could hear the fear in it.

"Real enough," she replied.

I wanted to run, but my legs felt heavy, like the night itself was holding me in place. The water was only a few steps away, its surface barely catching what little light was left.

"Why me?" I asked, and now my voice was shaking for real.

She tilted her head and looked at me with her hollow eyes. "Because you laughed at me," she said. "You mocked what you did not understand. Now you become part of my story."

Her small hand reached out and grabbed my arm. Her grip was firm, and I couldn't move. I couldn't scream. She started pulling me toward the water.

"You will not be forgotten," she said. There was nothing comforting in it.

Before I fully understood what was happening, I was under. The water closed over my head, cold and suffocating. Her laughter echoed around me.

As the water filled my lungs, I understood too late that Candle Face was real, and that I had just become part of her story.

When he finished, he thanked me for listening. Then, just as quietly as he had come in, he went back through the sunroom door and disappeared into the night.

I couldn't help but notice the way he kept coughing as he told his story. Each time he did, water poured from his mouth. It was hard to watch. He looked as though he was in pain, grimacing through nearly every word.

The fact that he was soaked made me wonder whether it really was rain. The amount of water coming from his mouth felt like a clue. Rain alone couldn't explain it. It seemed tied to the way Candle Face killed him. It was as if the water itself had stayed attached to his death.

IDENTIFIED? CANDLE FACE VICTIM #2: MAMA'S LAST EMBRACE

January 24, 2024

For the past three months, spirits claiming to be victims of Candle Face have been coming to me. Each one has asked for help finding their remains and identifying the people who killed them. I have done what I can, though; so far, I haven't been able to give them much closure.

That may be starting to change.

A former colleague of mine, a private investigator who worked missing persons cases with me, happened to see my appearance on the January 11, 2024, episode of *Beyond Believe Talk*, hosted by Beyond Believe Paranormal Investigators, where I spoke openly about these spirits coming to me.

Watch the *Beyond Believe Talk* podcast here: www.facebook.com/kimmikorpse/videos/337451305770787

Interested, he started looking into one of the cases on his own and turned up something that caught my attention. He focused on Victim #2.

I first encountered Victim #2 on November 18, 2023. She appeared to me as a young African American girl, around four or five years old. In her account, she said Candle Face lured her away from a swing in front of her mother's mobile home in Austin, Texas. She also spoke about missing her "Mama" and "Granny," and said she could still feel their love.

Using those details, my former colleague searched for missing children from Austin whose cases involved similar circumstances. That led him to the Charley Project website, where he found what appears to be a strong match: Tanisha Lorraine Watkins of Austin, Texas, who disappeared on January 5, 1984, at the age of two. According to the Charley Project, Tanisha vanished while playing on a swing outside her mother's mobile home. Her mother stepped away from the kitchen window briefly, and when she looked back, Tanisha was gone.

Read the Charley Project report about Tanisha Lorraine Watkins here: https://charleyproject.org/case/tanisha-lorraine-watkins

Tanisha's case closely matches the spirit's account:
1. Both involve a mobile home.
2. Both involve a child playing on a swing before disappearing.

3. Both point to a young African American girl missing from Austin, Texas.

4. In both accounts, the child disappears in the short moment when her mother turns away.

DESCRIPTION	MISSING PERSONS REPORT	SPIRIT'S TESTIMONY
Race	Black	Black
Gender	Female	Female
Age	Two years old	Appeared to be 4-5 years old
Missing location	Austin, TX	Austin, TX
Time missing	Winter	Winter
Hairstyle	Braided	Braided
Living condition	Lived in a mobile home	Lived in a mobile home
Relatives	Lived with mother and great-grandmother	Lived with "Mama" and "Granny"
Last Seen	While playing on a swing in front of a mobile home	While playing on a swing in front of a mobile home

These details line up too closely to dismiss. For the first time, I may have a real lead. Victim #2 may be Tanisha Lorraine Watkins. I can't say that with certainty yet, but it's the strongest connection I have found so far.

My next step is to look into this lead more carefully. If Tanisha is Victim #2, then there may be more to learn about what happened to her. Even if it means revisiting a very old case, it would move us one step closer to giving her, and possibly her family, some measure of peace.

After months of reaching out to paranormal investigators, mediums, and psychics, I have started to accept that I may not need to rely on them as much as I once thought. At first, I believed these cases would require the wider paranormal community. As I work through this, it increasingly seems the spirits may have chosen me for a reason, perhaps because of the skills I already bring to this. I have over three decades of intelligence and investigative experience.

Outside help still has value, but I'm prepared to carry most of this work myself. Many of the people in that world are busy with their own podcasts, appearances, and merch, and that limits how much time they give to real cases. I'm in a different position. I can put my full attention on these Lost Souls and on the clues they leave behind.

Even so, I'm still struggling with what comes next, especially if Victim #2 really is Tanisha Lorraine Watkins, a little girl who disappeared forty years ago. How do I even begin to think about contacting her mother after all this time? That isn't something I can simply show up and say at her doorstep. If I ever reach that point, it will require caution, research, and probably advice from professionals, including social workers, on how to handle something that sensitive with care.

The other option is to hold off on contacting the family unless I reach a far higher level of certainty about the spirit's identity. Emotionally, that may be the safer course. But it may also leave the spirit without the closure she's asking for. There's still a great deal I need to figure out. For now, I'll keep digging, follow the lead where it goes, and move carefully with each step, both for the spirits who have come to me and for the living people the truth may affect.

THE BETRAYAL OF THE PARANORMAL "EXPERTS"

January 29, 2024

In paranormal research, you would expect authenticity and courage from people who claim expertise. My recent experience has shown me something very different. What I've seen instead is cowardice, insincerity, and a blunt disregard for the truth. This entry comes out of my frustration with the so-called paranormal "experts" I turned to while investigating Candle Face, the ghost said to haunt the Austin area, and the one I have spent years naming, tracking, and writing about.

My path into this part of the investigation started with two interviews with people who claimed to know something about Candle Face. After those interviews, my nights filled with dreams of flashing lights and jarring sounds. Before long, those dreams changed. First came the screams. Then came clear voices and images of Candle Face's victims asking me to help them find their remains, identify who killed them, and connect with their living relatives. I believe these spirits chose me as their messenger because of my earlier confrontation with Candle Face, which I described in my memoir *The Empty Lot Next Door*, and because I know how to document what they are telling me.

Since October 2023, I have been visited by eleven spirits, each describing a violent death. I don't claim to be an expert in paranormal phenomena, so I reached out to paranormal investigators, mediums, and psychics in the hope that they could help me make sense of what I was dealing with. In spite of all their claims about courage and expertise, most of what I got from them was infuriating.

Many of these self-appointed investigators act fearless online, but their behavior says otherwise. At the slightest sign of actual paranormal activity, they run. Then, when confronted, they deny it, even when their own videos show exactly that. That kind of dishonesty destroys their credibility. It's also an insult to people who are actually looking for answers.

On January 24, 2024, I had a real break in the case when a former private investigator colleague connected the report of a missing African American girl to the testimony of one of the spirits. The moment I published a journal entry about that possible match, these "experts" suddenly cut ties with me. Their timing raises obvious questions. Are they jealous because I may have found more in a few months than they have in years? Or do they think I'm using these experiences for literary or financial gain?

There's another possibility that I think deserves closer attention. Fear. Across paranormal Facebook groups, Reddit pages, and even the Darknet, I have seen the same contradiction again and again. Many people in the paranormal community are drawn to the subject and still seem deeply afraid of the real thing. That fear shapes how they act and what they avoid. In Candle Face's case, I think that fear may explain a lot. She already has a bad reputation, and I have shared direct experiences involving her. For all their public talk about bravery, these experts may simply be afraid of crossing paths with something they can't control. That may be why they pulled away from me so quickly. They stay interested as long as the paranormal remains abstract, then retreat when it starts to feel real. That tells me a lot about how thin their courage really is.

Yes, I'm a writer, and that's probably one reason I was put in this position. My original research into Candle Face was meant for my blog. Once the spirits started coming to me, the focus changed. It became about their stories. If these experts had done even basic homework, they would know that. If the psychics are what they claim to be, they should have picked up on it immediately. Instead, they question my sincerity while profiting from their own work. They run podcasts. Some post YouTube videos with ads. Their websites sell merchandise, coffee mugs, shirts, handbags, crystals, tours, rentals, equipment, and whatever else they can attach to their brand. One of them is an author. But somehow, I'm the problem if I write a book that may help these Lost Souls. That is hypocrisy, plain and simple.

So here I am, left behind by people I thought might stand with me. Whether they're frauds or afraid, their behavior explains why they pulled away. The paranormal community has plenty of both. Either way, their actions have left me to keep going without them. The people who market themselves as experts in the paranormal often run from it. I'm still here, doing the work.

IDENTIFIED? CANDLE FACE VICTIM #11: THE GIRL FROM THE SHACK

January 31, 2024

I was contacted by someone who had seen my January 11, 2024, interview on *Beyond Believe Talk*, a podcast hosted by Beyond Believe Paranormal Investigators.

Watch the *Beyond Believe Talk* podcast here: www.facebook.com/kimmikorpse/videos/337451305770787

During that episode, I spoke about my childhood encounters with Candle Face and about the spirits of her victims who had been coming to me at night. These spirits had been asking for help locating their remains and identifying the people who killed them. The interview covered those visits, though it also included one strange moment when a psychic described Candle Face as a candle with a face that is "happy." Even so, I'm grateful I had the chance to speak about these spirits and the stories they wanted told.

The anonymous email I received focused on the spirit I referred to during the podcast as Victim #11. Her account was the hardest I have heard. She told me she was killed by her boyfriend and his friends after being drugged, assaulted, tied up, and raped, because of her disbelief in Candle Face. The email suggested a possible connection between her testimony and the real-life case of Roxanne Paltauf, who disappeared in July 2006 under circumstances that appear disturbingly similar.

The email included a link to a KVUE article published on January 24, 2024, just two weeks **after** the spirit's visit.

Read the KVUE article about Roxanne Paltauf here: www.kvue.com/article/news/crime/austin-cold-case-roxanne-paultauf/269-f520dfa4-aba3-4682-9d00-6da6b5a92751

The article does appear to line up closely with the spirit's account, but I still don't know whether the spirit and Roxanne are the same person. The possibility is serious, but my role here is still limited. Any connection like this has to be approached carefully. No one should be treated as guilty without evidence and proper investigation. Cases like this require real investigative work beyond a spirit's testimony. I encourage readers to do research, but the pursuit of justice must remain with law enforcement and the proper authorities.

Here are the similarities between the missing person report and the spirit's testimony.

DESCRIPTION	MISSING PERSONS REPORT	SPIRIT'S TESTIMONY
Race	White	White
Gender	Female	Female
Age	18	Appeared to be 18-20
Missing Location	Austin, TX	Austin, TX
Relationship	Boyfriend age 28	Boyfriend in the late 20s
Other	Family didn't approve of the boyfriend	Family didn't approve of the boyfriend
Last Seen	In a hotel room with her boyfriend	In a hotel room with her boyfriend

Personal Note to My Readers

I want to thank those of you who have supported this project and allowed me to give these Lost Souls a voice. Because of that support, they have at least been heard. That doesn't solve what happened to them. But after being silent for so long, being heard counts for something.

Still, we need to remember that what comes through from the spirit world is only part of the story. These accounts may offer leads, but they have to be handled carefully and checked against real evidence. We can't act on partial or unclear details alone. There are too many ways for the truth to be distorted. The spirit who came to me may not fully understand everything that happened to her. Candle Face may also be interfering. Even if the spirit resembles Roxanne Paltauf, it's still possible that some details belong to someone else, or that parts of the account were lost, altered, or confused.

That's why I'm asking you to approach this with care and discipline. Leave criminal investigation and legal action to law enforcement and other trained professionals. Our role is to listen, document, and advocate, not to take justice into our own hands.

If we handle this responsibly, we may be able to honor these spirits without crossing the boundaries of the living world and the law. That's how we keep moving forward without causing more harm.

CANDLE FACE VICTIM #13: BENEATH THE SURFACE

February 13, 2024

I'm sitting in front of my laptop right now, frozen. The glow from the screen feels almost hostile as the cursor keeps blinking at me, waiting. My hands are shaking so badly that it's hard to think straight, much less write. My mind feels locked in distress, and I'm waiting for some sense of calm to come back.

I went to bed early tonight, worn out from a day of yardwork and expecting a quiet night for once. The last three weeks had been still, and I had started to think the spirits were giving me space. There had even been some progress. We had a strong lead on Victim #11, and GenX Paranormal Investigations, a team out of the Houston area, was willing to look further into her case. That quiet ended tonight.

I must have just drifted off when I heard the floorboards creak, a sound I now associate with my nocturnal visitors. Before I could even sit up, I saw him. A man standing over me, soaked from head to toe. His hands were ice cold as he pinned my shoulders down. Then, without warning, he slapped me across the face.

What happened next was the worst thing I have experienced so far. He leaned over me and vomited into my mouth. The taste and the feeling of it were unbearable. I gagged and choked and tried to fight him off, but my strength went fast. Just as I thought I was about to black out, he stopped. Then he slapped me again and left me gasping.

He was furious. That much was obvious. He was angry because I had neglected his story, and then it hit me. He was the same spirit who had come to me in late December. I had promised to write down what he told me, but I never did. I put it off. In the weeks after, I only mentioned him briefly during a podcast. He made it clear that he had come back to force me to finish what I should have done the first time.

Here's his testimony:

> Under the Texas night sky, the boat rocked lightly on the dark water in the cove. My two sons were asleep on the deck. My wife had stayed behind with relatives, so it was just me and the boys on an overnight boat trip on the west side of Austin. The air was cool, the night was calm, and the city felt far away.
>
> I looked over at my boys while they slept and thought about how kids pick up so much from what we tell them. They wanted ghost stories. They wanted something creepy. I never believed in any of that stuff, so I usually brushed it off. Most of the time, I filled their heads with stories

about politicians and history because I thought that mattered more.

But one of my sons cut me off while I was in the middle of one of those stories.

"Please, Dad," he said. "Tell us a ghost story. We're out here in the dark. We want to hear about Candle Face."

His younger brother pushed himself up a little, holding his teddy bear and staring at me. I hesitated, then gave in.

"In the heart of Austin," I began, "there was a legend about Candle Face, a ghost who, people said, hurt anyone who didn't believe in her. But there was a boy named William who thought it was all made up."

My sons leaned in. They were paying close attention. But I didn't believe any of it. To me, it was just a story.

I kept going. I told them about William walking into the dark creek where Candle Face was supposed to live. The wind over the water sounded louder while I talked. I described the little girl with a face like melted candle wax, and William standing in front of her and saying, "I don't believe in you, Candle Face." Then the ghost wailed and vanished, and William walked away unharmed.

When I finished, my sons looked disappointed.

"Dad, that's not scary," my oldest said.

"Ghosts aren't real. Candle Face isn't real," I said. "Come on. It's time for bed."

Once they settled into their sleeping bags, I couldn't relax. I knew those waters well, and I got the urge to take a swim. So I slipped into the water. It was cold, and the cove was almost too quiet.

After a minute, I noticed something was wrong. The knot tying my boat to the dock looked loose. I swam toward the dock fast.

When I got there, I saw a pair of legs. Small legs. I looked up and saw a little girl standing there. Her hair hung down in long tangled strands, covering most of her face. When I finally saw her clearly, she looked burned. Her face looked like it had been ruined by fire.

It was Candle Face.

Before I could do anything, her hot, clammy hand grabbed my head and shoved me under the water. Panic hit me right away. I fought to hold my breath, but she was too strong. Just before I passed out, she pulled me back up, and I came up coughing and choking.

Then she spoke.

"You do not believe. But your life depends on it."

I was too scared and too confused to do anything but listen while she told me her story. She talked about betrayal, pain, and being left behind. She wanted to be acknowledged. She wanted to be believed.

"Believe in me," she said. "Believe, for your life depends on it."

Shaking, I said, "I... I can't."

Her grip tightened, and she shoved me under again. I panicked. I fought for air. I fought to stay awake. She kept pulling me up just long enough to make me suffer through it, then forcing me back under.

After a while, I started losing strength. She didn't stop. I had mocked her, and now I was living the story I had laughed at.

At the end, when I had almost nothing left, she held me under and didn't let me come back up. I felt the cold pull me down, and then everything went black.

When he finished, the spirit looked at me with a solemn expression. Water dripped from his mouth as he gave me one last warning: "Pay closer attention to your visitors. Another slip-up, and Candle Face will come for you. Her punishment will be far worse than you can imagine."

Then he turned and disappeared into the portal.

Personal Note to My Readers

This was a grim first for me. It was the first time a spirit had struck me. In the past, they had seemed wary of physical contact, but not this time. This time, I was hit twice and nearly drowned in what I can only describe as ghostly vomit.

Even after that, I'm grateful it didn't go further. I have seen what happens to people who ignore what Candle Face sets in motion, and I know tonight could have been much worse. I took this as a warning. I can't keep delaying these testimonies.

Candle Face doesn't leave room for hesitation. From this point on, I need to document every testimony as soon as it happens.

CANDLE FACE VICTIM #14: SOBRIETY'S TEST ON SIXTH STREET

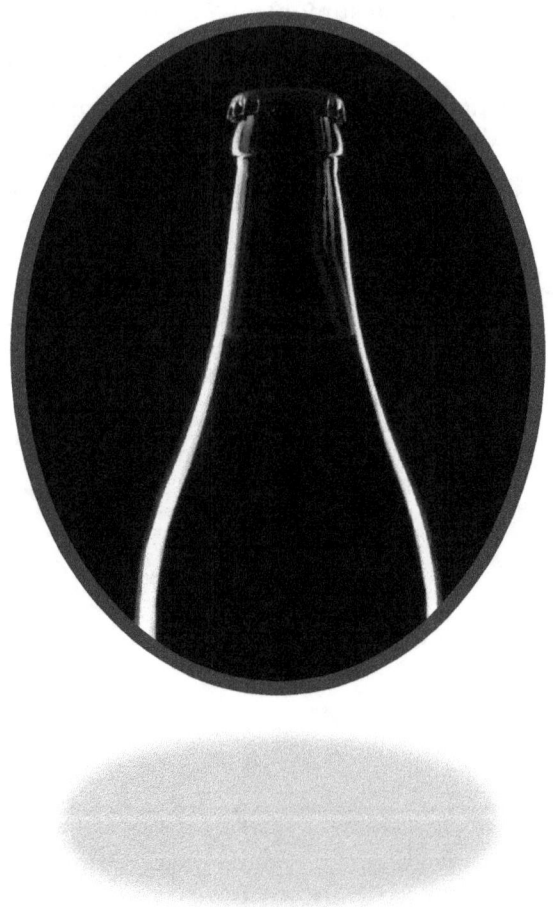

February 20, 2024

Last night, I got up for my usual middle-of-the-night trip to the bathroom. When I came back, a dripping-wet man was standing by the couch. He had a beer bottle in his hand, and I knew right away another spirit had come to tell me what happened to him.

I walked toward him and offered my hand, but he pulled back and kept his distance. I expected that, so I sat down and made myself comfortable, ready to listen. He looked ready to talk. Then he began.

The Texas sun was just starting to go down, throwing long shadows across Sixth Street. I stood there taking it in, feeling like I had finally done something I used to think was beyond me. I had gone months without a drink. I wanted to prove to myself that I could be around all of it, the bars, the music, the noise, the people drinking, and still not fall back into old habits.

The street was alive that night. Music poured out of doorways. People laughed. Even though I was there alone, I felt like I belonged. I played a few games of pool, got some street food, and for the first time in a long time, I was having a good time without alcohol.

Then things shifted. A group of kids came up handing out flyers like it was life or death. They had this look in their eyes, like they had seen something nobody else understood. I tried to avoid them, but one girl stepped in front of me. Tears were running down her face as she shoved a flyer into my hand and told me it would save my life.

I looked at it. There was a picture of a pretty little girl on it, and they said she was their mother. I didn't buy any of it. It looked like some strange cult thing to me. But the girl handing me the flyer looked desperate. She said something about punishment if I didn't believe. I shook my head and walked away, telling myself she was just having a bad night.

I needed to get away from the noise, so I headed toward Lady Bird Lake. It was quieter there, and the air felt cooler. It seemed like the right place to clear my head.

Then I heard it, a splash, followed by a child crying for help. I didn't stop to think. I ran to the water, kicked off my shoes, and went in. There was a little girl in the lake, struggling to keep her head up. I swam out to her, grabbed hold of her, and started pulling her toward shore.

Then she spoke, and everything in me went cold.

"Why did you save me? Take me back."

Her voice was wrong. It didn't fit her body, and there was something deeply wrong in the way she said it. I tried to calm her down, but she started pulling at me, dragging me back into the lake. She was far too strong, stronger than any child should have been.

Then her face changed, and I saw a girl with a burned face. My heart froze.

I tried to fight her off, but she wouldn't let go. She pulled a bottle from the water, it just appeared in her hand, and forced it against my lips. I begged her to stop, but she laughed. She tipped the bottle, and I couldn't stop her. I swallowed and choked on the burn of it while she kept laughing.

I don't know how long it went on, but I could feel myself going under. I was weak, and she was stronger than I could understand. As I went under, all I could think about was what people would believe. After everything I had done to stay sober, they would think I went back to drinking. They would think I lost.

Days later, they found my body. The papers said it was alcohol poisoning and that I must have fallen into the lake drunk. My friends and family mourned the man they thought I was. They never knew the truth. That little girl killed me, not the drink.

And that girl with the flyers, I still wonder about her. Does she think about me? Does she regret what happened that night? Or is she proud of it? It doesn't matter now. The regret belongs to me, and it's not leaving.

After he finished, he stepped back. He realized I was staring at the beer bottle in his hand. When he noticed, he explained, "This bottle's become part of me. It's a sign to everyone trapped in Candle Face's lair. It brands me as a drunk, a man who lost to his cravings." Then he took a sip, turned, and disappeared into the portal.

Personal Note to My Readers

While I listened to his testimony, I kept thinking about the girl handing out the flyers. Does she lie awake thinking about the people she believed she was helping? Or has she convinced herself their deaths were justified?

What happened to this spirit, a sober man whose death was made to look like a relapse, also made me think about everyone else who has crossed Candle Face's path. How many people left home one night and never came back, with no one ever knowing what really happened to them? And how many more may still end up in her hands, pulled in by a flyer and a warning they laughed off?

CANDLE FACE VICTIM #15: RETURN TO THE WATER'S EDGE

February 21, 2024

Another wet, Lost Soul came to me. It started with the sound of wet footsteps and water dripping onto my face, which jolted me awake. The moment I opened my eyes, he snapped, "Wake up, we're doing this now."

Still half asleep, I forced myself to sit up, rubbing my eyes and trying to clear my head. He stared at me hard. "You ready yet?" he asked, his voice full of urgency and irritation. I nodded because I didn't know what else to do. He wasted no time and went straight into his story:

> Downtown Austin at night isn't for the weak, and I lived on the edges of it, in the places most people avoided. Being homeless meant staying cut off from the rest of the world. Survival didn't leave much room for anything else. Days and nights ran together, and there wasn't much to laugh about. Mocking things, though, that came easy. That was how I dealt with life. It was my armor against how bad things really were.

> The stories about Candle Face, that ghost child, always made the rounds among the homeless. To me, they were just entertainment. I laughed at anybody who believed in her. Some burned-up kid haunting people because they didn't believe in ghosts? It sounded stupid.

> I had a spot near Town Lake [Lady Bird Lake], under Congress Avenue, where I could be alone and away from the chaos downtown. It was my quiet corner, and I didn't have to hear people talk about Candle Face like she was real. I made fun of them every chance I got.

> "Why waste time on that nonsense?" I would say, shaking my head. "A ghost kid? Come on, we've got real problems."

But one night, when fog started rolling over Town Lake, something shut me up fast. She appeared, a small figure stepping out of the mist. Her face was burned so badly it barely looked human.

"Why do you mock my pain?" she asked. Her voice wasn't loud, but it carried all around me. It had a strange sorrow in it that didn't sound like a child's voice.

I tried to brush it off. "You're not real. You're just some story people made up to scare each other." I even laughed, telling myself maybe I had had too much to drink.

But she kept coming closer. The air turned hot, and I couldn't pretend anymore. "I am as real as the suffering you live with every day," she said. "So why do you mock those who believe in me?"

I didn't know what to say. I shrugged and acted like I didn't care. "It's easier to laugh than to believe in ghost stories."

She tilted her head and looked at me like she knew more about me than I wanted her to. "You know what it feels like to be invisible, to go unheard. So why deny others their belief?"

"Belief doesn't put food in my stomach or keep me warm at night," I snapped.

After that, she started showing up every night. It didn't matter whether I wanted to see her. She was there. Each time I mocked her, she seemed more real. Other people noticed too. They started talking about me, saying I was losing my mind. "He's taunting her," they said. "She's going to get him."

And they were right.

The night it ended, she was waiting by the edge of Town Lake, half hidden in the fog. "Your mockery ends tonight," she said, her voice carrying over the water.

I felt heat in my chest, like something had grabbed my heart. I couldn't keep pretending anymore. "What are you going to do to me?" I asked, and my voice shook.

"You will see," she said. "It is time you understood the cost of your ridicule."

Before I could move, the ground beneath me gave way, and I went straight into the lake. The water was freezing. I fought to reach the surface, but something kept pulling me down.

I saw her under the water. Her burned face was right in front of me, and her empty eyes were fixed on me.

"Why?" I managed to choke out.

"Your mockery brought you here," she said, her voice calm and final. "You denied others their pain. Now you will face your own."

I tried to scream, but the water swallowed me. Everything went dark, and the last thing I saw was her fading away and leaving me alone in the cold.

They found my body the next day floating near the shore. The news talked about another drowning in Town Lake. The homeless community believed Candle Face was responsible. Candle Face had taken another victim, one who mocked her believers.

He finished his story and made a move like he was about to backhand me. I flinched, and he laughed, clearly enjoying it. Then he did it again. This time, I didn't flinch. I stood up and shoved him. To my surprise, I touched him. My hands hit his chest. It was the first time I had ever made physical contact with one of the Lost Souls. His eyes widened, and he let out a horrible, waterlogged gasp. I stepped forward and shoved him again, forcing him back toward the portal. Once he saw I was ready to do it again, he backed away and disappeared into it.

Personal Note to My Readers

Once he was gone, I ended up right back at my computer, feeling like I had to write down everything he said. But as I sat there looking at the screen, one question kept bothering me: why should I share this spirit's story at all? The truth is, I don't feel any sympathy for him. A part of me thinks he deserves to stay in Candle Face's lair. My first reaction was anger, and if I'm being honest, some satisfaction at shoving him back. Looking back, part of me thinks I should have done more than that.

Even so, I'm writing it down. Maybe that comes from responsibility. Maybe it comes from trying to make sense of him and

Candle Face and the way they connect. Either way, I decided to record every word. Whether I like it or not, this story still needs to be told.

CANDLE FACE AND AUSTIN'S SERIAL KILLER RUMORS

February 23, 2024

As the person these spirits turn to when they want their final accounts told, I have become an unwilling recorder of the dead. Lately, a troubling pattern has started to stand out. The last three spirits who came to me all drowned. Each one said Candle Face was responsible. That has pushed me to look more closely at the thread connecting their stories.

At night, I sit at my desk and go back through what they told me. Each account ends in water. Each one ends with drowning. That raises a hard possibility: Candle Face may be tied to the series of drowning deaths in Austin.

As I looked into the history of the waters where these deaths happened, I found a generational divide in what people call it. Older

Austinites still call it Town Lake, a name tied to an earlier version of the city. Newer residents usually call it Lady Bird Lake, after Lady Bird Johnson and her environmental work. Even that split in naming says something about Austin's shift from a college town into a much larger city.

Then there are the serial killer rumors. Despite police efforts, these drownings remain unsolved, with no clear link except what the spirits themselves have described. One spirit told me he jumped in to save what he thought was a drowning child, only to be pulled under by Candle Face.

As I compare these accounts, the pattern becomes harder to ignore. She keeps showing up in the same place in these stories, whatever the true source behind her may be. Every victim had dismissed her legend. Then each of them died. That raises the possibility that Candle Face is more than local folklore and that she may be targeting skeptics and doubters.

Skeptics see it differently. One University of Texas professor I spoke with, who asked not to be named, offered another explanation. "The human mind seeks patterns, attributing unexplained tragedies to folklore. It may be a coping mechanism rather than evidence of the supernatural," he said. Even so, the overlap between the legend, the real deaths, and the warnings from the spirits gives me enough reason to keep looking.

Through my writing, I'm trying to understand their world, even when the spirits themselves are hostile. It's difficult work, but I don't see another path. These nocturnal visitors chose me, and I'm trying to understand what Candle Face's role may be in the rumored serial killings that have hung over Austin.

My purpose is to record these stories, honor what these spirits say they endured, and examine this part of Austin's history as carefully as I can. If I can bring even a little clarity to something clouded by fear and rumor, and if that helps prevent more deaths in the waters of Town Lake (my preferred title), then the project is worth it.

INSIDE CANDLE FACE'S LAIR

February 25, 2024

At night, when everything is quiet, I get no peace. The spirits of Candle Face's victims keep coming to me, telling me how they died and asking for help. In the beginning, their stories came in pieces. Now I remember them clearly. But tonight, something changed. Candle Face herself took me into her lair.

A wave of heat came over me as I drifted into the shadow portal in my living room. For the first time in four decades, Candle Face stood in front of me. The wax-faced figure I had imagined as a child had become something worse than anything I had pictured. The name I gave her as a boy now felt childish compared to what she really was. Her face was a mass of charred flesh, twisted like melted wax. Her eyes were hollow pits lit by a wicked glow. Her voice was rough and raw, like it had been burned down over years of smoke and heat. Every

130

word came out through breath so hot it felt dangerous. Her skin hissed and popped like oil over a flame, and the air around her felt close to catching fire. She was no figment. She was real, and so was the dread that came with her. As she led me through her lair, her blackened face and scorched body stood as a warning of what waited there.

"Ray," Candle Face said, her voice carrying around us, "you have been chosen. Chosen to witness this and chosen to act. Look at what becomes of those who remain here."

As we walked, I saw thousands of souls. Their faces were twisted in torment. Their bodies were held by something that looked like invisible chains burning into them. The air tasted like ash. Sorrow hung over everything. The heat coming off her body seemed to poison the whole place.

"Why me?" I asked. "You put them here. You could end this. Why would you put that on me?"

"Why me, you ask? Why do all of you ask that?" Candle Face answered, laughing. "But you are different, Ray. You faced me before and came out alive. Very few can say that. Your resilience impressed me. So did your ability to put horror into words." She fixed that empty stare on me. "The way you wrote about me in *The Empty Lot Next Door* was flattering, other than the silly name. You have a gift with words, Ray, a power that rivals mine with souls. That is why you were chosen. Our shared history. Your fight. Your victory. You beat me once. That makes you suited for this. You understand the fear, the pain, and the cost. Who better to help them than someone who has faced me and won?"

The thought that my earlier encounters with her, and the fact that I had survived them, had led to this moment felt like a challenge I never wanted. I had been dragged into a fight I never asked for. The path ahead was dangerous, and it was clear my history with Candle Face was nowhere near finished. Still, somewhere under the fear, something in me pushed back.

Then Candle Face laughed again, and there was nothing human in it.

"Ray, you still do not understand the game. Yes, you beat me once. Very few can say that. But do not make the mistake of thinking that means you can do it again. Their torment feeds me. It is my power. And you, without meaning to, have become useful. Your efforts to help them only stir things up and make their suffering worse. That is the irony. If you keep trying to save them, you deepen their pain. If you walk away, you doom them and yourself in another way. The rules are not the same now. Beating me once was your miracle. Thinking you can repeat it is your mistake. You are in my world now. Here, I do not lose."

Her words were meant to trap me. I had beaten her once, and it had nearly destroyed me. Now she was using that history against me, admitting it while trying to break my confidence. But the fact that she admitted I had beaten her at all gave me something to hold onto. If I had done it once, then she wasn't beyond being challenged.

What was becoming clear was worse than a simple haunting. Candle Face was using my need to help these spirits against them and against me.

As we kept moving through her lair, her threat became even plainer.

"Help them, Ray, or join them," she said. "And if you join them, your punishment will be crafted with such care that what you have seen here will seem minor beside it."

I woke drenched in sweat, my heart pounding as if I had been running. The dream felt too vivid to dismiss. I made my way to the computer to write it down, but when I sat there, misery hit me all at once.

What had I become? A vessel for the dead. A man hounded by spirits and now threatened directly by Candle Face. My attempt to help the Lost Souls had become its own kind of curse. Walking away offered no comfort. It only made the whole thing feel darker.

At my lowest point, I questioned everything. My sanity. My purpose. My place in any of this. The shadows in the living room, where the portal opens, seemed to mock me. For a moment, I thought about suicide. Just for a moment. I wanted the torment to stop. Death felt like the only way out.

But that passed. Defiance came in behind it.

I couldn't let Candle Face win. The spirits who had come to me with their stories deserved better than to remain pieces in her game. I owed them something. I owed myself something.

So I started writing.

As I wrote, another thought took shape. Candle Face had shown me all of this for a reason. She wanted exposure. She wanted her story told. She wanted the stories of her victims spread too. She wanted me to be the one to do it.

That changed how I saw this. She was trying to use me. She wanted me to help build her legend. She wanted me as her mouthpiece for the Lost Souls and her messenger at the same time.

But that cuts both ways.

If Candle Face wants her story told, then I can tell it on my terms. I can tell what she is, what she does, and what her victims have endured. I can also tell the stories of those who resisted her, those who didn't give in quietly, those who still push back even from inside her lair. She may want exposure, but exposure can work against her too.

That realization changed the shape of this fight for me. Helping the Lost Souls is still an act of mercy and resistance.

Candle Face thinks she handed me a role in her plan. Maybe she did. But in doing that, she also gave me a way to fight back. She wanted me to become a tool for hopelessness. I don't intend to give her that.

I know now that my role is to keep telling the truth about what she's doing. For the Lost Souls, for the people still living under her shadow, and for myself, I'll keep writing.

Candle Face may want attention. She may want fear. She may want the world to know her name. Fine. But if I tell her story, I'll also tell the stories of those who suffered under her and those who fought back. I'll tell the truth about her cruelty. I'll tell the truth about the damage she leaves behind. And I'll not let her control the meaning of those stories.

As I kept writing, I felt less alone. The thought that other people might read this and decide not to look away gave me something solid to hold onto. I know what lies ahead will be dangerous. I know Candle Face and whatever serves her will not make this easy. But this is about refusing to let her define the whole story.

One thing I do know is this: I'm not alone. My readers and I are tied together in this whether we wanted it or not. There is strength in that. There has to be.

So I'll keep going. For the Lost Souls. For the living. For myself. I'll use words the only way I know how.

Candle Face wants her story spread through me. In her arrogance, she may have handed me the very thing that could work against her. I'll tell her story, and the stories of the Lost Souls, in terms she can't control.

Who's with me?

I'm asking that plainly now. If Candle Face wants to spread fear, then the answer has to be people willing to stand together against it.

I plan to write more often about Candle Face, about what she has done, and about the Lost Souls still trapped in her lair. I'll keep sharing these testimonies through every outlet I can use, books, podcasts, interviews, the website, whatever helps get their stories in front of people.

I'm still moving forward. The question is whether others will move with me.

Visit me at www.candleface.com and take part in the investigation.

CANDLE FACE VICTIM #16: A WAITRESS' LAST WALK HOME

March 1, 2024

I used to go to bed early every night, hoping a Lost Soul would show up. Lately, though, they have become more aggressive. Some have even attacked me. The rush I once felt has given way to responsibility. I know I have to help them, whatever that ends up costing me.

Tonight, while I was working in my garage, the door suddenly lifted on its own. First, I saw a pair of legs. Then a bluish miniskirt. Then a white T-shirt stretched over a slim frame, topped by long blond hair. This spirit wanted my attention before I fell asleep right then. Once she stepped inside, the garage door shut behind her on its own.

She started to speak, but I cut her off and asked, "Can I ask you something?" She looked stunned, and so was I. It was the first time I had tried speaking directly to one of these nighttime visitors. I have tried touching them before, but they always pulled away. In a shaky voice, she answered, "I can't answer questions." Knowing what might happen to her when she went back through the portal, I didn't press it. "Okay," I said, and she continued, pacing through the garage as she told me what happened.

Working as a waitress on Sixth Street in Austin was always chaos, late nights, loud crowds, and no shortage of stories. One of the stories that kept coming up was Candle Face. People said she was the ghost of a little girl who went after anyone who didn't believe in her. I had heard all of it before, locals telling stories, tourists trying to scare each other, and I never gave it much thought. To me, it was just another story.

At least that's what I thought.

The night everything changed started like any other shift. I was pouring drinks, clearing tables, and catching pieces of conversations as I moved through the room. People were talking about Candle Face again. Some of the regulars described her as a vengeful spirit with a burned face who punished doubters. I laughed with one of the men at the bar and said, "If Candle Face is real, I guess I'm next!"

I didn't think about it again as I walked home later that night. The streets were quiet. Then, without warning, the air around me turned hot, far hotter than it should have been. That was when I saw her.

She stepped out of the shadows, a small figure not much taller than a child, her face badly disfigured. Her voice cut through the silence. "You mock what you do not understand."

I froze. My heart was pounding. "W-w-who are y-y-you?" I stuttered, even though I already knew.

"I am the truth," she said. "The belief you scorn."

Now, I can see her clearly. Her face was charred and misshapen, like something out of a nightmare. I wanted to tell myself I was seeing things, but deep down I knew who she was.

"You... you're not real," I shouted, my voice shaking.

She moved closer. "Your disbelief gives me strength," she hissed. "Your mockery invites your end."

Panic hit me, and I tried to run, but I couldn't move. It felt like hands were holding me in place. Her laughter filled the street. "You wanted proof? Now you will be part of my story."

And that was the end of it.

The next week, the bar was full of rumors about me. I had vanished without a trace. My coworkers were confused, and the last person to see me, the regular I had joked with, kept talking about how I had laughed at the Candle Face story just hours before.

Now they tell my story the same way they used to tell hers. My joke turned into a warning for anyone who thinks they're safe. And she doesn't care whether you believe. She'll make you believe.

If I can tell you one thing, Ray, it's this: don't laugh at her. Don't doubt her. Believe, even if it's only to keep yourself alive.

She thanked me for listening, and I managed to say quietly, "You're welcome." She looked startled, as if she still couldn't believe we had spoken to each other out loud. Then the garage door opened again, and she slipped out. I ran to my computer and wrote down everything I could before any of it faded.

CANDLE FACE VICTIM #17: TAKEN FOR NOT BELIEVING

March 4, 2024

I think I finally fell asleep sometime around 4:00 a.m. after hours on the couch scrolling through Facebook and watching YouTube videos. Then my house alarm went off and snapped me awake. In the confusion, I saw a man standing there in khakis and a button-down shirt. He started talking immediately, not giving me any time to wake up fully or collect my thoughts.

> In Austin, people talked about Candle Face like she was real. I never bought any of it. I was a software engineer. I trusted systems, logic, and things I could test. Ghost stories belonged to bad sleep, stress, or people seeing what they expected to see.

My encounter with Candle Face began like any other night. I was buried in work, with nothing but the light from my screen filling the apartment. Everything felt normal until the room grew hot. At first, I ignored it. Then I checked the thermostat. Then I saw her out of the corner of my eye.

She was standing there, small, burned, and impossible. Her face looked as though it had been ruined by fire, and her eyes were fixed on mine. I froze.

"Why do you keep rejecting what is right in front of you?" she asked, her voice calm. Too calm.

I shook my head and tried to hold on to reason. "Ghosts aren't real. You're not real. You're stress, lack of sleep, something in my head."

"Am I?" she asked. Her voice stayed even, but there was something sad in it, as if she had heard that answer too many times. "You dismiss anything you cannot explain."

I stood up, hoping movement alone would break whatever this was. "You're a myth. A story. That's all."

She stepped closer, and the heat in the room intensified. "Your disbelief does not erase me," she said.

I turned back toward my computer, trying to shut her out. "You're not real," I said, though I could hear the weakness in my own voice.

She laughed, low and soft. "You will learn soon enough," she said.

I didn't sleep that night. Every time I closed my eyes, I felt watched. I kept seeing her face, burned and twisted. The shadows in my apartment seemed to move on their own. Even the silence felt wrong.

The next day, I tried to put it aside, but something had changed. I kept looking over my shoulder. I checked the thermostat twice. I walked through the apartment. I told myself there had to be a reason for what I had seen. It still got to me.

Then it got worse. Objects in my apartment started shifting. Bursts of heat came out of nowhere. And her voice kept following me. "Why will you not believe what you see?" she would ask again and again, as if she meant to wear me down.

I started staying out as late as I could, wandering around Austin just to avoid going home. But she followed me there too. She was always somewhere just beyond sight, there enough that I felt it and still couldn't prove it.

One night, I finally reached my limit. I was exhausted, scared, and desperate for some answer. "What do you want from me?" I shouted into the empty apartment.

She stepped out of the shadows as if she had been waiting for that question. "Belief," she said. "Say I am real. Admit what happened to me."

I shook my head, still clinging to the last bit of logic I had left. "I can't believe in something that makes no sense."

Her expression shifted. She looked angry.

"Then you leave me no choice," she said.

The walls of my apartment disappeared, and Austin was gone. I was somewhere else, somewhere empty and burning hot. She stood there with a faint glow around her, her hollow eyes fixed on me.

"Where am I?" I asked, my voice shaking.

She tilted her head. "Where the ones who deny me end up."

Panic took over. "Let me go. I'll believe, I promise!"

Her eyes narrowed. "Too late," she said.

I tried to run, but there was nowhere to go. She moved toward me, her burned hands reaching out.

"Please!" I begged, fear finally breaking through everything else. "I believe in you. I do!"

She didn't stop. Her hand touched my face, and it felt like fire tearing through me. I screamed, but there was no one there to hear it.

After that, I was gone. They found my apartment untouched, but there was no sign of me. People around here still talk about it. The ones who believe in Candle Face say she took me for not believing.

Without another word, he turned, walked back into the dark corner of my living room, and disappeared. I checked my surveillance footage afterward, but there was no sign of him.

CANDLE FACE VICTIM #18 AND #19: THE WALKMAN LEFT IN THE ROAD

March 8, 2024

My plans for an evening walk got wrecked by a sudden wave of pollen, so I got on the treadmill instead. It's in the sunroom, angled near the same corner where Victim #7 and Victim #12 once appeared. As I started slowing down for my cooldown, I heard soft sobbing coming from that corner. When I looked over, I saw two faint figures, a man and a woman.

I stepped off the treadmill, but before I could speak, the woman said, "Please, keep going. I miss the days when I could run. I miss it so much." I gave her a small smile, then walked over to the sofa and sat down, quietly motioning for them to come closer. They stayed where they were, standing side by side and holding hands. Then she began her story:

My last day alive is burned into me, every step of that winter run, every moment that led to the end. I had my Walkman strapped to my arm, and my favorite songs were drowning out the cold and everything around me. Music made me feel safe. It made me feel like I was sealed off from the world.

That ended when a car slowed down next to me. A young guy leaned out and asked for directions. I was so caught up in the music and the rhythm of my run that I didn't hear him at first. I had to pull off my headphones to understand what he was saying.

At first, it felt normal. Then he asked whether I wanted a ride. I said no. Before I could react, he grabbed me. It was fast, violent, and sudden. One second, I was running along the side of the road. The next, he was shoving me into the trunk of his car. My Walkman hit the ground, and the music cut off. The silence that followed made everything feel even more real.

He drove off, but a few minutes later, he came back. I could hear him outside, moving slowly, like he was in no hurry at all. He was looking for the Walkman. I guess he noticed it when I dropped it. He picked it up, but he left the battery case and the batteries behind, scattered on the road like they meant nothing.

I didn't know it then, but Candle Face had sent him. He was supposed to take me somewhere secluded in the woods as part of whatever plan she had. But he didn't follow through with that part. He killed me right there instead. Maybe he wanted control. Maybe he just couldn't stop himself. Whatever the reason, he disobeyed her, and that sealed his fate.

Candle Face doesn't forgive disobedience. She came for him too, and now he's trapped here with me. She bound us together, literally. Our hands are fused. I feel him every moment, and it's unbearable. I hate him, and I'm trapped with him with no escape. Not yet.

Ray, if you want to help, you need to find the battery case for my Walkman. The battery case and the batteries are still out there somewhere along that lonely road where he grabbed me. Trace the path of my last run in the Georgetown area. Somewhere along that stretch of road, my body is still waiting to be found. If you find it, maybe I can finally be free of him. Free of Candle Face.

Thank you for listening.

She gave me a knowing smirk, thanked me for listening, and then stepped back into the portal, her killer following close behind, their hands still joined.

Personal Note to My Readers

The young man, who helped bring about his own end without realizing it, is now trapped with her in Candle Face's lair. There's a hard kind of justice in that. The room went quiet, and I caught myself giving a faint, dark smile at the thought of his shock when he learned he would be bound to the same punishment he forced onto his victim.

That reaction felt honest, even if it was cold. As I keep replaying the encounter, I can still feel that hollow, dark laugh sitting in my chest. It feels closer to accepting the twisted justice of what happened to him.

But my heart still aches for her.

CANDLE FACE IS REAL, AND SHE'S HERE TO HELP

March 11, 2024

    Yesterday, I received an interesting email from someone calling himself "Sammy." He says he speaks to Candle Face by the creek, the same place where I used to get ambushed on my way to school. In his email, he described one-sided conversations he believes he has with Candle Face while walking his dog. The fact that this same creek appears in both his account and my own history makes it hard for me to dismiss. It may be one of the places most closely tied to her activity.

    Here is what he wrote in his email:

Hey Arthur,

For the purpose of this email, my name's Sammy and I live near the creek where you say Candle Face hangs out. I've been reading your articles about her and, dude, I gotta say, I'm totally on board. I walk my dog, there every evening, and sometimes we just stop on the bridge. I kinda talk to her. I never hear her talk back or nothing, but I feel her answers in my gut.. Like this one time, I asked if she was sad, and the wind picked up real quick like she was saying, "Yeah, kinda." Another time, I was stressed about work, and I swear the water in the creek got all calm all sudden, like she was telling me to chill out.

I think it's cool you're writing about her, Arthur. More people need to know she ain't just some scary ghost – she's got this kindness. Like, she really wants to help us out. I tell all my friends about her, trying to spread the word. Some think I'm just making stuff up, but others, they get real interested.

Now, here's the crazy part I gotta tell ya. Last week, I was at the creek, and this shadow comes out nowhere, right next to me while I'm talking to Candle Face. I don't see this shadow any other time, just when I'm there talking about serious stuff, like asking Candle Face to help with with bullies. It's like this shadow understands me and Candle Face? I got this weird feeling it's Candle Face in another form, just checking in.

But hey, if you want use this in your blog or something, that's cool with me. Just don't put my email out there. It's a fake one anyway, haha. We got to keep spreading the word about her, showing people she's not what they think.

Keep doing what you're doing, Arthur. Candle Face needs more believers, and what you're doing could really help her find peace or whatever it is she's looking for. And maybe, just maybe, we can make our neighborhood a better place, knowing there's someone like her watching over us.

Thanks for listening, man. And remember, not everything you

hear about ghosts is meant to scare you. Some of them, like Candle Face, they're just misunderstood.

Later, Sammy

Sammy's account differs from the stories I usually receive. In his version, Candle Face is misunderstood and may even be capable of empathy. That possibility complicates the picture.

I have been asking myself whether I should share experiences like his. It seems worth including perspectives that might add to what we know, but I also have a responsibility to stay as factual and measured as I can, especially when so much of what we know about Candle Face comes through personal experience rather than anything that can be independently verified.

How do we handle testimony like Sammy's in a way that stays grounded and still respects the darker accounts others have shared? The best answer may be to present these stories as personal accounts while keeping them separate from the investigative side of this project.

I would like to hear what you think about that. How do we make room for experiences like Sammy's and still keep this project grounded? I also found myself thinking about something else. A few days ago, I wrote about exposing Candle Face's evilness. That's still important. If there's another side to her, I shouldn't ignore it. Sammy would probably agree.

Please share your thoughts at my website: www.candleface.com.

IDENTIFIED? CANDLE FACE VICTIM #18: THE WALKMAN LEFT IN THE ROAD

March 16, 2024

On March 8, 2024, two spirits visited me, a woman and a man. To my surprise, the woman told me the man standing beside her was her killer. She said Candle Face had punished him for disobeying her orders. According to the woman, Candle Face meant for him to take her to a remote place in the woods, but instead, he killed her outright. Candle Face then killed him in return. Now they're bound together, forced to remain hand in hand until her remains are found.

She shared one detail that may be especially important. After he abducted her, he put her in the trunk of his car and drove off. Then he came back for the Walkman she had dropped during the attack. He found it in the road, picked it up, and left again. She said the batteries and battery case from the Walkman were still there at the abduction site, and that finding them would lead to her remains.

A week later, on March 15, 2024, someone left a comment on my blog, which I call my "Journal," saying that these two Lost Souls may be tied to a missing-persons case in Georgetown, Texas. The missing person is Rachel Cooke. That caught my attention. I looked into Rachel's case and found several disturbing similarities that line up with the spirit's testimony.

DESCRIPTION	NEWS MEDIA REPORTS	SPIRIT'S TESTIMONY
Race	White	White
Gender	Female	Female
Age	19	19-20
Missing Location	Georgetown, TX	Georgetown, TX
Activity when Missing	Jogging near parents' house	Jogging
Last Seen	January 10, 2002	Winter
Other	Jogging with a pink or yellow Walkman	Jogging with a Walkman
Other	Witnesses saw a vehicle driving slowly in the area	The killer drove slowly into the area to look for the missing Walkman

There's a large amount of information online about Rachel Cooke, including social media pages devoted to finding her. KVUE, an ABC affiliate in Austin, is one of the outlets that has covered her case. Their reporting states that Rachel, who was a cross-country runner, a sport I also enjoyed when I was younger, disappeared while jogging along Neches Trail near her parents' home in Georgetown, Texas.

Read the KVUE report here: www.kvue.com/article/news/local/missing-for-18-years-in-search-of-rachel-cooke/269-5750e8b9-e4c6-4af9-bcd5-d75c4b971648

Another report, from the *Austin American-Statesman*, says Rachel had a yellow Walkman with her during that final run. Although there have been persons of interest over the years, no arrests have been made, and the case has remained unsolved for twenty-two years.

Read the *Austin American-Statesman* report here: www.statesman.com/story/news/crime/2021/01/10/williamson-sheriff-has-new-suspect-case-missing-rachel-cooke/6615785002

Could the spirit who came to me be Rachel Cooke? The similarities are striking, but I want to be careful here. The spirit's account lines up with several parts of Rachel's disappearance, though many missing persons cases share overlapping details, and it would be a mistake to force a conclusion too early.

For now, this lead needs further investigation. In the meantime, I strongly urge readers not to contact Rachel Cooke's family directly about this. It's a sensitive matter, and any further steps, if they're warranted at all, should be handled by qualified professionals.

CANDLE FACE VICTIM #20: LED INTO THE WOODS

March 18, 2024

I had grown tired of sleeping on the couch, so I went upstairs to sleep in a real bed. As I climbed the stairs, I noticed the faint outline of a man standing in the bedroom. I wasn't sure whether he might turn aggressive the way some spirits have before, so I moved carefully and pushed the door open a little farther. He looked almost as uneasy as I felt, and that eased me some. I stepped inside and leaned against the wall without saying anything. He seemed to take my silence as permission to go on, and he started to speak.

> I thought Candle Face was just another urban legend, until I learned she was real.

I never walked right after the accident. The limp stayed with me. So did a lot of other things. Part of me never really came back after that crash. Sometimes I would catch myself talking under my breath just to remind myself I was still here.

Most nights, I stayed downtown, hanging around the edges of things. I never felt like I belonged anywhere, but watching people come and go was enough to pass the time. That's where I met her, my "Lady Friend." That's what she liked me to call her. She had a laugh that sounded warm at first, but there was always something off about it.

She was obsessed with the stories people tell about Austin, especially Candle Face. Every time she brought her up, you could see it in her face. She came alive talking about the woods in northwest Austin and the thing people said was waiting out there, something with a face like melted wax and fire in its eyes, going after the people who doubted her.

"You don't believe, do you?" she'd ask, half teasing, half serious.

I'd laugh and shake my head. "Nope. I believe in what I can see and touch. Stories are just stories."

She never liked that answer.

One night, she took my arm and led me away from downtown. We caught a cab to the northwest side of town, and from there she walked me into the woods. She barely said a word, but the way she held onto my arm told me this wasn't some casual walk.

"Why are we here?" I asked. I could already hear the nerves in my own voice.

She turned and smiled. "You'll see. I'm going to show you something real. Then you'll believe."

The trees started closing in around us. The trail got tighter the farther we went.

Then we came to a creek. The water was dark and still. That was when I saw her. Candle Face.

She stepped out from the trees like she'd been standing there the whole time. Her face looked twisted, like melted wax. Her eyes burned low like candles. Then she reached for me with a hand that shouldn't have been solid, but was. I tried to pull away, but I was too late.

"Thank you," Candle Face said to my Lady Friend. Her voice sounded like dry leaves moving across the ground.

Then my Lady Friend laughed. It was wild and wrong, nothing like the laugh I thought I knew. "You should have believed," she said.

I panicked and tried to get loose, but Candle Face already had me. With my limp, there was no way I was going to outrun her. She dragged me deeper into the trees. The branches seemed to close in around us until all I could hear was my own fear.

Pain shot through my leg when I stumbled, but worse knowing my Lady Friend had handed me over. The person I thought I knew had led me straight to her. Candle Face had become real to me. I felt it in my chest. I felt it in my leg. I felt it in every step she forced me to take.

As she dragged me deeper into the woods, her eyes dimmed a little, almost like she was satisfied. Then she said, low and steady, "Belief is the beginning and the end. Only when you believe do you truly see."

And in that last moment, I saw.

The spirit started to reach out his right hand, then quickly pulled it back and glanced toward the portal as if he knew he had made a mistake. I didn't press it. I thanked him for his time and told him I would try to help him. He looked surprised, almost as if he had not expected me to say anything. Then he winked and limped back into the shadows of my bedroom.

Personal Note to My Readers

It looks like I have started speaking directly to the Lost Souls. This may be the second or third time it has happened. When they tell their stories, I still mostly listen. I don't ask questions yet. Once they're gone, I always wonder why I can't bring myself to ask them anything in the moment. I hope that changes. I have a long list of questions I want to ask, but right now, I still can't do it.

This makes me think about the confrontations I had with Candle Face as a child. At first, she got into the house through unlocked doors, so I started locking them. Then she used open windows, so I shut and locked those too. My family made fun of me for it, but I kept doing it anyway. Eventually, I realized I could control parts of the dream. In one encounter, I saw Candle Face outside a window trying to open it. Even though I knew I was dreaming, I rushed to lock that window. As soon as I did, she moved to another one. By staying ahead of her, flying from window to window and locking each one, I kept her from getting in. It ended in a major confrontation once I figured out how to shape the dream itself. I'm hoping I reach that point with these visits from the Lost Souls. I have too many questions left unasked.

CANDLE FACE VICTIM #21: LURED BY THE DRUMBEAT

March 22, 2024

Just as lightning lit up the sky again, followed by thunder so sharp it felt as though it cracked right in front of me, a shadowy figure slipped into my upstairs bedroom while I was getting ready for bed. I knew what he wanted. I said nothing. Something in me knew I needed to listen. Without a word from either of us, he began to tell his story:

> I used to find peace in my walks. They gave me a way to get away from everything for a little while. Everything out there seemed to have its own rhythm, and my drum was always with me. That drum was more than an instrument to me. It was my voice. I spent hours trying to pull out the perfect beat, the one I felt somewhere deep in

me. No matter how hard I tried, it always stayed just out of reach.

Then one day, I heard it.

It was late fall. I had stopped for a moment after seeing a snake move through the grass when I heard the sound. A drumbeat. Pure, perfect, alive. It was the rhythm I had been chasing my whole life, the one I'd dreamed about but never managed to make real.

I followed it without thinking. I pushed through the brush, desperate to find whoever had mastered what I couldn't. The sound drew me farther and farther into the woods, each beat pulling harder than the last. Then I stepped into a clearing, and the drum stopped.

Three figures were waiting for me.

I should have turned and run. I didn't. I couldn't move. They weren't drummers, and they weren't there to teach me anything.

"You have failed her," they said together.

The air turned hot. That was when I understood they were servants of Candle Face. She'd already given me a task, and it was an ugly one. She wanted me to bring her the people who doubted her, the nonbelievers. But I couldn't do it. I couldn't hand innocent people over to her and know what would happen to them. I thought I was doing the right thing.

The figures moved closer. The ground split under me and gave way. The earth swallowed me. When I opened my eyes, I was in her lair.

Candle Face stood in front of me, her face like melted wax, her eyes burning with anger.

"You spent your life chasing the perfect beat," she said, her voice crackling like fire. "Then I gave you one thing to do, and you refused."

I tried to speak. I tried to explain. Nothing came out.

"You chose them over me," she said. "Now you stay here with the souls you failed to protect. You will watch their suffering and know it is because of you."

I thought I was saving people. I thought I was keeping them from her. Instead, I only added to the number of souls trapped there.

Now the world I knew is gone. The walks, my drum, all of it is far away. Her lair is my prison. And the sound of that drum, the perfect beat I chased for so long, still follows me. I hear it just at the edge of hearing, always out of reach, always there to remind me of what I lost.

I thought I could stand against her. I thought refusing her would count for something. I was wrong. Now all that's left is failure.

He stopped there. Then he looked at me as if he wanted to say more but couldn't.

When he was gone, I kept thinking about what he had said. If his account is true, then Candle Face is hunting skeptics and punishing those who refuse to serve her. That changes the picture. It means some of the souls trapped with her may have died because they refused to obey her. Doubt was no longer the issue.

That leaves me with the same question I keep coming back to: where do we go from here? How do we help these Lost Souls and keep Candle Face from taking more lives?

I don't have a full answer yet. With each account, it becomes clearer that Candle Face's power is stronger than I first thought. If there is any chance of helping these souls or understanding how she operates, then the stories need to be documented, examined, and shared carefully.

That is part of why I keep directing people to www.candleface.com.

It's one place where information, theories, and possible leads can be gathered in one spot. If Candle Face depends on fear and confusion, then careful documentation may be one of the few ways to push back.

I'm asking people to take this seriously. Share what you know. Compare details. Look for patterns. Help where you can. Candle Face has already taken too many.

CANDLE FACE VICTIM #22: BENEATH THE I-35 OVERPASS

March 27, 2024

I was stretched out on the couch, thinking about how often the Lost Souls had been showing up. Lately, none of them had acted hostile toward me. Maybe that meant nothing. While I was getting the couch ready to sleep on, the side door swung open, and a strong wave of body odor came in with it. A man, somewhere around my age, stepped inside. His eyes went straight to the fresh brownies my wife had made a few hours earlier. I offered him one. What surprised me most was that he answered. "I appreciate the offer, but taking part in the pleasures of the living isn't something I can do without consequences." I smiled and said, "Well, if you change your mind, they're there." We moved into the living room, and for the first time, one of my nocturnal visitors sat down. Curious, I asked, "What brings you here tonight?" This is what he told me:

I used to stand on a corner downtown with my torn sign, just another face in the homeless crowd. My days went in circles: ask for change, buy a drink, numb the pain, do it all again. It was the life I had, and I lived it.

One day, a man came up to me holding a flyer. His eyes had a strange intensity to them, like he was trying to sell me something bigger than what was in his hand. The flyer showed a drawing of a little girl. She looked sad, almost forgotten, like she was waiting for someone to notice her. She looked like she might have been from Mexico or Central America. He told me she could save people like me and give me a way out of the hell I was living in.

I didn't take him seriously. What good is a savior when your stomach is empty and the cold is cutting through you? I threw the flyer back at him and said, "I need food, not another savior."

That night, I crawled under the I-35 overpass, where I usually slept. My mind went back to that man and what he said about the little girl. I couldn't decide whether it sounded like hope or desperation.

The next morning, an older man, one of the regulars on the street, came up to me. He had a look in his eyes like he had seen something he couldn't forget. He warned me to stay away from the little girl because she was really Candle Face. He said nothing good came from crossing paths with her. But his warnings only made me more curious.

Over the next few weeks, I couldn't get her out of my head. At first, I blamed the alcohol. The voices I started hearing had to be from drinking too much. But they didn't stop, not when I was sober and not when I was drunk. They whispered things to me, secrets, promises, and they made everyday life harder to bear.

Eventually, I connected with a few other people who had also heard of Candle Face. We traded stories and tried to piece things together. We thought we were getting close to something, but the truth always stayed just out of reach.

Then came the betrayal.

The man who had handed me the flyer was working for her the whole time. He had been leading us to Candle Face all along. One by one, my friends fell under her spell. The noise in my head got louder and louder until it pushed me to the edge.

I thought I could take it, but I couldn't. One night, I drank more than I ever had, hoping to shut everything off. I thought I was taking control. That was when she came to me. Candle Face herself.

She stepped out from behind a pillar, her face dimly lit, like melting wax with two flickering flames where her eyes should have been. Her voice was calm and cold. "Do you still not believe?" she asked.

I laughed without any humor in it. "You're just in my head," I said. "A drunk's nightmare."

She shook her head. "No," she said. "I have been waiting for you to give up. Now you are mine."

In the end, I gave up. I let her take me. My spirit was too tired to fight anymore.

Now my old street corner belongs to someone else, another Lost Soul who doesn't know what's coming. Candle Face's power keeps spreading. She keeps pulling people like me under. The world keeps moving and doesn't notice. Meanwhile, the homeless, the forgotten ones, keep dying.

And me? I'm just another name on her list. Another warning no one will hear.

He finished his story, then walked over to the brownies. The smell had clearly been pulling at him the whole time. I sat there and watched as he stood near them, his whole posture full of wanting. At last, he turned to me. "I'd give anything to taste the life I once knew," he said quietly, "but sometimes it's better to leave certain wants unfulfilled." Then he walked out of the house. By the time he reached the sidewalk, he had already started to fade into the night, until nothing was left but the sound of a tired sigh.

Personal Note to My Readers

One detail in his story that really interested me: the flyer with the drawing of a little girl. He said she looked sad, almost forgotten, like she was waiting for someone to notice her. He thought she might have been from Mexico or Central America.

That makes me wonder who she was. Was she only an image meant to draw people in, or was there something more behind it? The spirits often leave pieces of themselves inside the stories they tell. This may be one of those pieces.

I don't know what it means yet, but I'm keeping it in mind as these visits continue.

THE FIRST DIRECT CONVERSATION
WITH A LOST SOUL

March 27, 2024

My house, on the outskirts of Houston, has become a stop for spirits looking to be heard. I've always tried to offer them a quiet corner of my home and a listening ear, but until now, it's felt like a one-sided interaction. Tonight changed everything.

The night was thick with the scent of freshly baked brownies, a warmth that seemed to spill over into the spirit world. The side door eased open. It was Victim number 22, a middle-aged man whose gaze fell immediately upon the brownies set out on the kitchen counter. Our exchange began simply.

"Would you like some?" I asked.

He responded in a calm, measured tone, "I appreciate the offer, but partaking in the pleasures of the living isn't something I can do without consequences."

That was the moment it hit me. This was the first time a Lost Soul addressed me so directly. I was actually having a conversation. I've wished for this moment, yet never truly thought it would arrive. Now that it's here, I feel a surge of hope. If this visitor could speak so openly, maybe others will follow suit. Maybe I can truly help by listening to their stories and following the clues they leave behind.

I recently posed a question to several paranormal Facebook groups, wondering if direct interviews with spirits were possible. The answers were mostly skeptical. People suggested tools like Ouija boards or spirit boxes, methods I don't find helpful in my situation. As it turns out, the real key might just be talking, like you would with anyone else stepping into your home.

Of course, it's not all excitement. Communicating with these spirits feels like crossing into dangerous territory. They've spoken of boundaries and consequences. I'll need to tread carefully, respecting both their world and mine. Now I have something more solid to work with. This feels like a turning point. I can respond to these spirits, speak with them, and maybe offer real help.

I've been given the chance to help these souls find answers, and that's given me a clearer sense of purpose. If talking is what opens up their stories, then I'm prepared to listen all night long.

I know the journey ahead is far from over. Candle Face is out there, and this newfound communication could put me at greater risk. The scent of brownies still hangs in the air, and with it comes the feeling that I may finally be on the right track.

As long as these spirits come knocking, I'll keep opening the door. The only way to learn about Candle Face and bring peace to these restless souls is to keep listening.

INSIDE CANDLE FACE'S LAIR

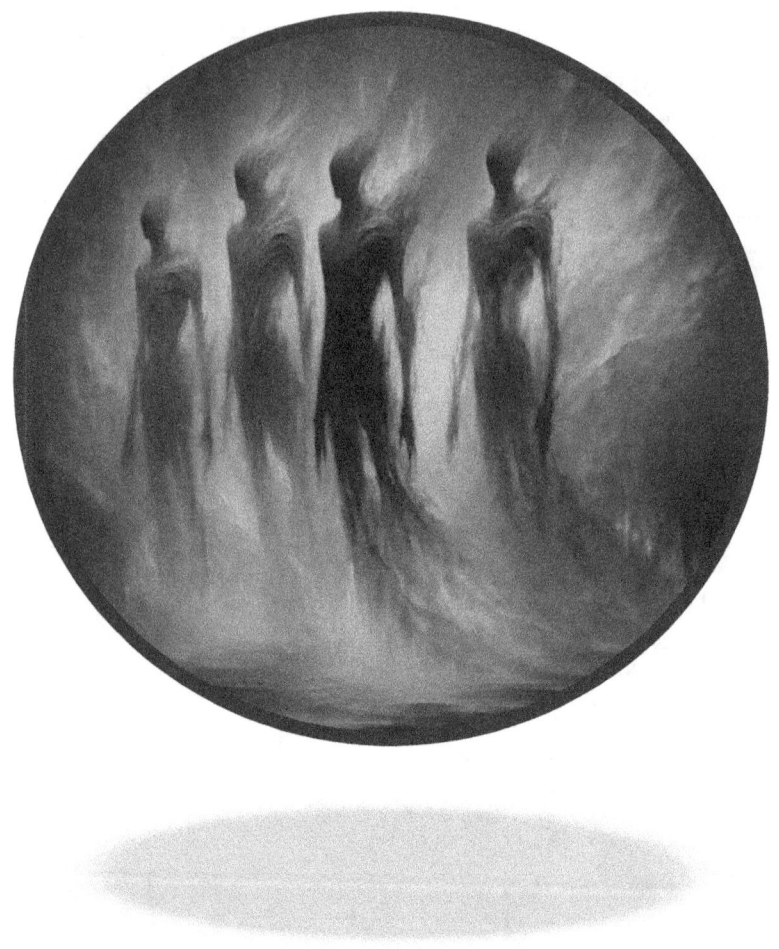

March 28, 2024

    As dusk turned into night, I lit a candle. Its light threw long moving shadows across the room. I settled into my massage chair, thinking about which spirit might come next and what I might ask now that I seemed able to speak to them directly. I closed my eyes. I had no idea I was about to face the worst thing I had seen yet.

The air turned hot. The candle flames twisted into ugly shapes. Then Candle Face herself appeared. Her face seemed to melt in front of me, and flames flickered inside the hollows where her eyes should have been.

She didn't speak at first. She only stretched out one sizzling hand. The wax-like skin pulled longer than it should have, wrapped around me, and held me in a crushing grip that felt like fire. In an instant, my living room was gone. I was back in her world for the second time. Her lair. Her hell.

Candle Face was furious. She accused me of crossing a line between the living and the dead. The Lost Soul, Victim #22, who had spoken to me the night before, had broken some forbidden rule, and Candle Face held me responsible. She meant to show me the damage I had done while believing I was helping.

Her lair stretched out like an endless abyss. Everywhere I looked, I heard the cries of her victims. The air stank of decay. Candle Face led me through it again, and the only light came from her burning form.

With each step, the horrors became worse. Spirits were trapped in devices that made no sense and offered no mercy. Their bodies were twisted, stretched, bent at impossible angles. Their screams filled the air. Dark shapes, most of them roughly human, seemed to power those devices and feed off the pain they caused.

In one part of her lair, the Lost Souls were hunted by shadows that took the shape of their worst fears. Giant spiders with glowing eyes. Ghostly figures whose faces twisted into warped versions of loved ones. Beasts and things that seemed built only to attack the mind.

The souls ran twisting paths that led nowhere but back into the hands of those fears. There was no rest. No way out.

In another part of the lair, the Lost Souls stood in a silence more disturbing than screaming. Their mouths were sewn shut. They were forced to watch the worst moments of their lives replay over and over like a film with no end. Shadowy figures yelled cruel truths and lies into their ears, stories of how their lovers had moved on, forcing them to watch their husbands and wives having sex with their new lovers while the world of the living forgot them. It wore at their sanity and left them desperate to scream, to beg for mercy that would never come.

Further in, other spirits were trapped in mirrors. But the mirrors didn't show them as they were. They showed monstrous versions of them, loaded with every guilt, shame, and regret they had carried in life. The mirrors made every small failure look unforgivable. Every insecurity became something grotesque. The souls tried to look away, but the mirrors always moved back into view.

Then I saw Victim #10. The woman who had mocked Candle Face and shown off her devil tattoo. Now she was trapped while shadows wearing the faces of her old companions circled her and jeered. They flaunted marks like hers, all of them burning, as if the symbol she had used in defiance had become part of her punishment.

Not far from that, I saw Victim #18 and Victim #19. They were trapped in a constant replay of their last meeting. The woman who loved to run was caught in an endless sprint, her Walkman filling the air with bleak music. The man who killed her was forced to follow close behind, horror all over his face as he faced the reality of their fused hands and joined fate. Shadow figures chased them, shaped by his guilt, his fear, and what he had done.

I realized then that these souls were there for Candle Face's amusement. I couldn't escape the thought that my efforts to speak with these Lost Souls had somehow helped put them in deeper torment.

In another part of the lair, I saw a worse cycle still. Some spirits were forced to relive their final moments again and again, each time with more pain than before. Victim #11, the woman from the shack, was made to relive the repeated rapes, the betrayal, and the knife going into her chest, only for it all to begin again just as life left her body. Nearby, a man died in a burning building over and over, the flames taking him each time, only for him to be restored so it could happen again.

This was Candle Face's hell. It was a place of pain she ruled with pleasure. Her laughter moved through the caverns, stripped of anything human. As I watched it, I felt hopeless. I understood. This visit was a warning. A look at what waits for anyone who interferes in her affairs.

Then Candle Face turned that fury on me.

"Foolish mortal," she said, and the ground shook. "You dared trick one of my Icnopilli into answering you directly, breaking a silence that has governed the dead for ages. Did you think your actions meant nothing? Did you think you were saving them? Your ignorance has done real damage. Your need to interfere feeds their suffering. Every Icnopilli that came to you for relief has now been cast deeper into torment because of what you did."

She towered over me. Flames moved where her eyes should have been. Hot drops from her sizzling skin struck my face.

I wanted to answer her. I wanted to argue, to beg, to explain. I couldn't get the words out.

"You have not helped," she said. "You have harmed them. You have condemned them. And now you will see the agony you caused.

You will carry it."

In that moment, I understood what she was accusing me of. I could see why Candle Face was angry. I had tried to do more than listen, and I had crossed into something I didn't understand.

"You thought you could investigate me. You thought you could speak for the dead," she said. "You are a rift, Ray. Your presence brings ruin."

Then she was gone.

Standing there in her lair, surrounded by everything I had seen, I felt the force of it settle into me. The screams. The torment. The possibility that my attempts to help had only made things worse. Her words felt like a verdict.

And I thought about the Lost Soul who had stood in my home a few nights earlier, looking at the brownies on the counter. He had been a man broken by homelessness and addiction, then pulled in by the false promise of salvation. The man who had first approached him with stories of Candle Face had been one of her followers, using the desperation of the homeless to draw them in. That detail now looked even worse. Candle Face was a predator who used suffering as bait.

Now, after seeing her lair, I heard it as proof that she feeds on the weakest places in people and waits until they have nothing left.

Then I thought about his last words to me when he refused the brownies. "Sometimes it's better to leave certain wants unfulfilled."

I should have listened more carefully to what he was really saying.

This visit changed something in me. It showed me how dangerous this new ability to speak with the Lost Souls really is. In trying to offer comfort, I may have dragged them into deeper torment. That realization is enough. I won't try to question them again. I have already done too much damage.

Personal Note to My Readers

During that encounter, Candle Face used a term I didn't recognize. I wrote down what I thought I heard, then spent hours trying different spellings based on the sound of it. At first, I didn't know what language I was dealing with. I searched phonetic variations, compared dictionary entries, and kept narrowing the possibilities until the trail started pointing me toward Nahuatl. That led me to the Online Nahuatl Dictionary hosted by Wired Humanities Projects, where I found this entry: https://nahuatl.wired-humanities.org/content/icnopilli. The word was *icnopilli*, glossed there as an orphan, a fatherless child, or a person deserving of compassion.

That definition caught my attention for another reason. Mr. Smoe described Candle Face as compassionate. At the time, I didn't know what to do with that. I saw too much cruelty in her for that word to make sense. After finding *icnopilli*, I had to ask whether this was the kind of compassion he meant. Was her compassion tied to the abandoned, the broken, and the dead in some older, harsher way?

I can't say that one word proves exactly who or what Candle Face is. Still, if I heard her correctly, this may be the first real clue I've found to her origin. It may point to something much older than I first believed.

CANDLE FACE VICTIM #23: THE PREACHER WHO LOST HIS FAITH

April 2, 2024

I'm slumped on the couch tonight. I'm tired, tired of these nightly visits from souls in torment. I'm starting to think I'm not who they need anymore. Maybe it's time to stop. Candle Face must be pleased, using my weaknesses against me so easily. I feel spent, and whatever faith I had in myself is running low.

Just as that hopelessness was about to take over, I heard music drift through the room. It came from the far corner, and when I looked, I saw a figure stepping out of the portal. He was dressed like a man of the church, but an inverted cross hung around his neck. He motioned for me to stay quiet, as if he wanted only my attention.

So, I said nothing. My heart was pounding when he began to speak.

I thought my faith was unshakable. I built my life on it, helping people through the worst moments of their lives and always telling them, "Never lose faith." It was part of who I believed I was. But I never imagined that faith would be tested this way.

One evening, after a late service, I was on my way home when I felt it. The air was too warm. I tried to ignore it, but then she appeared.

She stepped out from behind a flickering streetlight. Her face was burned, hollow, and twisted. But it was her eyes that struck me most. They seemed to look straight through me and pull at something deep inside.

Fear took hold of me, but I held to my faith. It was all I had.

"I don't fear you," I said, trying to sound brave.

At first, she only stood there and watched me. Then she spoke, her voice low. "I come to challenge your faith."

That was how it started, our nightly arguments. She used scripture like a weapon, twisting it to weaken what I believed. "Even Satan disguises himself as an angel of light," she said one night. "How can you trust what you see or what you believe?"

I answered her with the words of Christ. "Blessed are those who have not seen and yet have believed."

Every time she came back, she pressed harder. "Why do you cling to faith when it blinds you to suffering?" she asked. "Faith without works is dead."

I answered as best I could. "Let your light so shine before men, that they may see your good works and glorify your Father which is in heaven."

But her words began to work on me. Doubts I had never allowed myself to entertain started pushing in. She found every weakness in me and kept pressing until it opened wider.

Then one night she asked the question that finally broke me. "If God is for us, who can be against us?" she said, and her form grew larger, more threatening. "Yet here I stand, against you. Does that not make you wonder?"

And it did.

"I... I don't know," I said.

Her smile twisted with triumph. "Then you are mine."

I felt it in that moment, a burning pain in my chest, as if my soul were being torn open.

She broke my faith from the inside.

Now I'm trapped in her lair, tending to a different flock. The Lost Souls here still look to me for guidance, but the sermons I give are no longer about God. Candle Face twisted my role. Now I preach her mercy, a dark promise and the only comfort she allows me to offer.

The man I was is gone. What I regret most is losing my own faith and pulling others down with me.

She let me see my church one last time.

I sat in the pews, a spirit unseen by the congregation that once looked to me for guidance. The church that had once held hope and light now felt weighed down by grief and doubt.

I listened to them speak.

"He seemed troubled," one said. "Like he was fighting demons."

"His sermons lost their fire," another said. "It was like he doubted the very words he was preaching."

Their voices filled the church with disappointment, betrayal, and disbelief. "He led us to believe, only to lose his own faith," someone said.

My death left division behind where unity should have been. The church that had been my life's work now bore the mark of my failure.

As the vision faded, the last thing I saw was the empty pulpit. In it, I saw everything I had lost: my faith, and the trust and hope of the people I had led.

> Now I'm another soul in her collection, a preacher turned into a pawn, forced to serve the evil I once stood against.
>
> I used to think my faith couldn't be broken. Now I know how fragile it was.

After the preacher finished, he began to fade back into the corner he had come from. Before he disappeared, he paused and looked back at me one last time. I could see conflict in his face, resignation mixed with some last trace of duty. He told me quietly that he hadn't abandoned his calling as a preacher. In Candle Face's lair, he still tended to a flock, the Lost Souls.

He admitted that his sermons had changed into something terrible. He now preached Candle Face's mercy to the souls trapped there, presenting her as a kind of dark savior. Hope was gone, so he gave them the only comfort Candle Face allowed, telling them that only she could offer some warped form of salvation. That's how completely Candle Face can twist a person.

Then he stepped into the portal and disappeared. All I could do was stand there and try to take in what I had heard. A preacher who had once lived by faith was now forced to comfort the damned under Candle Face's rule. That alone showed me how far her power could go.

Personal Note to My Readers

A preacher who had built his life around leading others toward spiritual light found himself standing face-to-face with Candle Face. His faith was tested, and in the end, he lost his life along with the certainty he had always carried in what he believed.

Candle Face used doubt against him and took his soul. When his faith gave way, she twisted his role into something ugly, forcing him to preach her name as a source of mercy in a place where mercy doesn't exist. That's one of the clearest examples yet of how she works. Her violence reaches beyond the body. She goes after what holds a person together.

Still, facing something like Candle Face isn't as simple as telling yourself to believe harder. She uses fear, doubt, and even sacred words against people. Any real resistance has to start with knowing your own weaknesses.

That's what makes the preacher's story so painful. Even when we question ourselves or lose our footing, we still have to hold on to whatever keeps us tied to good. Sometimes that may be the only thing left between us and something like Candle Face.

I don't think doubt can be avoided. But it can't be surrendered to, either.

IDENTIFIED? CANDLE FACE VICTIM #13: BENEATH THE SURFACE

April 14, 2024

My encounters with the spirit world aren't slowing down. Today, I received interesting feedback about Candle Face Victim #13. A commenter suggested that the nocturnal visitor who came to me in late December 2023, and again on February 13, 2024, might be William Crumpacker from Lake Travis, Texas.

That tip led me to search online for "missing person Lake Travis late 1990s." I found a KXAN article titled "Unsolved: The Mysteries Lurking in Lake Travis," which described several drownings, including the disappearance of William Crumpacker in 1998.

Read the KXAN article here: www.kxan.com/news/unsolved-the-mysteries-lurking-in-lake-travis

He was a Dell marketing manager who vanished under unclear circumstances after going for a late-night swim from his boat in Little Devil's Cove while his children slept on board. His body was never recovered.

Read more about William Clark Crumpacker here: http://trackmissing.org/Cases/Details/913

The name William matches the one the spirit used in the ghost story he told during a boating trip, the same night he said he encountered Candle Face and drowned. Could the spirit who visited me really be William Crumpacker?

In late December 2023, a spirit came to me whose appearance and account lined up with those details. Unfortunately, I didn't document his testimony the first time. When he returned in February 2024, he was furious about that failure. He struck me twice and forced vomit into my mouth until I finally wrote down his story. I also shared pieces of his first visit on January 11, 2024, during an interview on *Beyond Believe Talk*.

Watch the *Beyond Believe Talk* podcast interview here: www.facebook.com/kimmikorpse/videos/337451305770787

Now, as the visits continue, I keep asking myself the same question: was that spirit really William Crumpacker? And if it was, what am I supposed to do with that? Direct communication has become dangerous because of Candle Face's warnings, and I'm not eager to risk more harm by pushing further.

So I'm turning again to my readers. Have you had any encounters with Candle Face? Have spirits ever come to you demanding recognition or acknowledgment? If they have, what happened? Any story, detail, or lead may help me understand what I'm dealing with and what may still be waiting in the darker corners of this house.

CANDLE FACE VICTIM #24: BURIED BENEATH THE HOUSE

April 15, 2024

After spending too much time scrolling through Facebook and YouTube on my phone, I finally set it down and got ready to sleep on the couch again. I walked over to turn off the light. When the room went dark, the brief flash from the switch showed a shadowy figure standing there. I froze and stared at the outline, with the sense that he was waiting to see what I would do.

Maybe he noticed my hesitation, because he moved closer and leaned against my bar. I couldn't make out much in the dark, but I saw two knives stuck in him, one through the chest and another at the neck. He looked toward me and spoke in a wet, blood-thick voice. "Looks like I've overstayed my welcome in the living world, don't you think?"

I didn't answer. I was aware that speaking might draw him deeper into Candle Face's lair. He didn't seem bothered by my silence. He stayed where he was, resting against the bar with those knife handles catching the faint light. Then he began to tell me how he died.

I used to think I had a decent sense of who I could trust. That morning proved I was wrong. It started before sunrise when my cousin and his friend pitched me a plan. We would drive to Houston, pick up a load of weapons, and sell them back in Austin. "Easy money," my cousin said, like it was nothing.

We left Austin that afternoon and took Highway 183. When we got to Luling, my cousin said we needed to stop and pick up a "box of gats." We turned off onto Salt Road and drove a few more minutes until we pulled up to a plain-looking house.

Something about that house felt wrong. The second we stepped inside, I knew I should never have come.

The betrayal happened fast.

I never saw it coming. My cousin hit first, driving a knife into my ribs and then into my chest. His friend followed with a blade to my neck. In those last moments, I saw their faces. Grim. Set. No regret in them at all.

They buried me beneath that cursed house. From under the floorboards, I listened while they talked through the rest of what they had planned. They were going to Houston to pick up the weapons, then north on Interstate 45 to some apartment to get more. After that, they'd head to San Antonio on I-10 and dump my belongings somewhere to throw off any investigation. Then they'd come back to Austin and act like nothing had happened.

But that house had something wrong with it long before they ever dragged me inside.

It wasn't long before Candle Face called them back. I watched them return and stand in that haunted spot above my body. She was already there.

Her voice filled the house, low and mocking. "You thought you could decide his fate without me?"

My cousin tried to act tough. "We did what we thought was necessary. He wouldn't have believed in you anyway."

Candle Face laughed again, lower this time. "Belief," she said. "People hand it over so easily, and it still carries power." Then she looked at me, even though I was already dead. "And you doubted me."

I found my voice then. "I never believed in the paranormal. I believed in what I could see and touch."

Her smile twisted. "And yet, here you are," she said. "Touched by the very thing you denied."

Then she told us the town and the house sat on old ground, a place tied to whatever lies between worlds. What they did to me there finished some kind of summoning.

She turned back to my cousin and his friend. "You share a name I know well," she said. "That tells me something about you. I see what use I can make of you."

They looked at each other, and I could see it on their faces. They knew they were in deeper than they had expected.

Then Candle Face softened her voice in a way that made it worse. "You did well bringing him to me," she said. "Now go find more like him. Doubters. Deniers. Bring them to me, and you stay in my favor."

They nodded. Fear and ambition did the rest.

Then she turned back to me. "As for you," she said, "yours ends here. Theirs is only starting."

Pain tore through me harder than anything I'd ever felt. I was bound to that house, one of many souls trapped beneath its floorboards.

And my cousin and his friend? They walked out with a new purpose. Their job was to feed others to Candle Face. They thought they were in control, but they were just pieces in her game.

Now the house above me stands like a tomb. My cousin and his friend may think they got away clean, but I hope their turn comes. Candle Face doesn't let anyone walk away untouched.

He gave me a sly grin, pushed himself off the bar, and stepped back into the corner. The knife handles in his chest and neck bounced with every step. Just before he disappeared, he gave me that same sneering smile and said, "Good luck, Ray."

Personal Note to My Readers

The accounts I have been hearing lately are different from the ones I documented earlier. This spirit gave unusually specific travel details: Austin to Luling, then Houston and San Antonio. He named Highway 183 and Interstates 10 and 45. He mentioned "Salt Road" in Luling. From a quick search, I couldn't find a road by that exact name, though there is a Salt Flat Road. That could mean his memory was fading, or it could mean something in the account was distorted.

What troubles me most is his claim that Candle Face described the town and house as an old site of power, and that multiple victims may be buried beneath that house. If that's true, it raises serious questions I had no chance to ask him:

- What exactly is this so-called sacred ground?
- Is there a pattern of unsolved deaths tied to that location?
- How does Candle Face fit into whatever happened there?

The killers, a cousin and a friend, were said to share the same name, and Candle Face seemed to see that as significant. Whether that's a coincidence, I don't know yet.

As more clues come in, I want to stay focused on what can be checked. Every detail, even the strange ones, may help us identify that house on Salt Flat Road.

CANDLE FACE VICTIM #25 AND #26: THE PEN PAL LETTERS

April 17, 2024

I arrived in Sugar Land, Texas, for a conference late that evening, much earlier than I expected. Traffic wasn't nearly as bad as I feared. Since I had time to spare, I stopped at Schlotzsky's for a quick meal. Afterward, I still had an hour or more to kill, so I sat in my car and planned to watch puppy videos on YouTube until it was time.

Then it happened.

While I was scrolling through my phone, the locked passenger door suddenly swung open. A young woman in her twenties got into my car without hesitation. My first reaction was fear. I thought I was being robbed, until I saw that half of her head was gone. In that instant, I understood. She was another visitor, and she had come to tell me what happened to her.

She didn't look afraid, and she didn't look hostile. She only looked at me with tired eyes, the kind that had seen more than I could understand. Then she started to speak, and I sat there in silence, waiting for whatever she was about to tell me.

This is her story:

Living in Austin, a city full of myths and legends, I had always been a skeptic. Out of all of them, Candle Face amused me the most. To me, she was just another story people told to scare kids or fool gullible adults. I never thought my disbelief would be tested.

It started with my secret pen pal in San Francisco. We didn't use Facebook or social media. We wrote letters. We'd been writing each other for years about our lives, our hopes, and sometimes our fears. But after a while, something in her letters changed. They started taking on this unsettling tone. She kept bringing up ghosts, vampires, and other things like that.

One day, she wrote to me about the Bloody Mary ritual, something I'd heard about a hundred times growing up. I brushed it off, played along, and even tried it myself in front of the bathroom mirror. Nothing happened, of course, and I laughed at how ridiculous it felt.

But as the months passed, her letters got stranger. She wrote more and more about the supernatural. She described things she said she'd seen, things she said had happened to her. The way she wrote started building this picture of a world where folklore and legend had real power, and it felt like she was getting pulled into it.

Then one evening, I got a letter from her that felt different from the rest. Her handwriting, usually neat and careful, looked rushed and shaky. She begged me to find information about Candle Face, the ghost of Austin, and send it to her. It was like she thought learning more about Candle Face would explain whatever had started haunting her.

I should have taken it seriously. I made things up. I thought it would lighten the mood. I wrote her a letter full of fake details and creepy made-up stories about Candle Face, like it was all some joke.

I filled that letter with made-up legends, each one worse than the last. I described Candle Face as a vengeful spirit hungry for the souls of skeptics. Then I mailed it.

Two weeks went by without another letter from my pen pal. I started to worry. I started thinking maybe I had gone too far. So I walked to the post office to send another letter, this time admitting that everything I'd written about Candle Face was fake.

On the way home, I kept thinking about her and how she seemed to be slipping deeper into those fears. While I was lost in thought, I ran into a boy I'd known in high school. We started talking, and it came easy, almost too easy. Before I knew it, hours had passed.

As the sun got lower, he offered to walk me home. It was kind of him, but I wanted to be alone for a while. I wanted the quiet of the woods near my neighborhood, the place that had always felt safe to me. So I told him I'd be fine and went to a clearing in the woods that I'd always thought of as my own.

I sat on a familiar log and thought about my pen pal again. I wanted to write to her about the boy I'd just seen, about something normal and hopeful, something that might pull her away from all the darkness she'd been feeding. I wanted to remind her there was still beauty in the world outside myths and ghost stories.

But that night, the woods felt wrong. They felt alert, like something was waiting for me. Then I heard faint voices. I couldn't make out much, just words like "Believe" and "Accept." I didn't know what they meant. I tried to tell myself it was my imagination.

Then a warm gust of wind moved through the trees. I turned, and what I saw filled me with dread.

Standing there was Candle Face.

She looked worse than anything I had ever mocked or imagined. Her face looked like it was melting, like wax running down from a flame. In that moment, I understood the stories hadn't come close to what she really was. And I understood something else. She was there because of me.

"Are you going to kill me?" I asked. I could hear the fear in my own voice.

"Yes, of course," Candle Face said, laughing.

"Why?" I asked.

Her mouth curled into a cruel smile. Her voice rasped like dry leaves dragged across stone. "Because, little girl, you mocked me. You denied my existence. You used me in your joke and wrote lies to your pen pal. Your inventions brought me here."

"I'm sorry. I didn't mean it. I thought it was harmless," I said, panicking.

"Sorry means nothing," she said. "There are enough true horrors about me already, and you still chose to invent more. There is no need for false stories. Every lie invites disbelief. Every joke weakens the fear I feed on."

Then she leaned closer, and her face seemed to melt faster as she got angrier. "Your pen pal," she said, "she feared me. She respected me. Her fear fed me well, and so did her body. But you mocked me in your letters. Now her soul belongs to me, twisted by the true stories I whispered to her at night, stories untouched by your foolish little inventions."

"What did you do to her?" I shouted.

"I told her the truth to fight your lies. Now she entertains my shadows. She is bound to me forever, and it is because of you."

Then Candle Face moved even closer. "And you," she hissed, "will join her soon enough. The two of you will scream together while the shadows have their way with you. Your secretions will soak into the soil of my underworld and draw even more shadows to you."

She pressed her mouth to my right ear and whispered, "And your screams, there will be many. The shadows will enjoy every one of them."

I started crying then, because I understood what I had done and what was about to happen to me. Candle Face shoved me off the log until I was on my back, my legs thrown up, helpless under her strength.

Then, calm as could be, she picked up a large rock. She raised it over my head while laughter filled the air. When it came down, death came with it. But not before I felt the shadows spreading my legs. They were already waiting for their turn.

She finished her testimony so quietly that I almost missed her last words. She asked if she could stay a little longer. She told me that when she was near me, the shadows couldn't hurt her. I said nothing. I knew too well that answering might draw Candle Face's anger onto her again. I can only hope she understood why I stayed silent. She opened the car door, stepped out, and walked toward the dark shapes waiting for her near the restaurant dumpsters until she was gone. I could hear the shadows shrieking with excitement as she disappeared.

Personal Note to My Readers

I'm asking again for help. So far, we have only managed to help four of the twenty-six Lost Souls who have come to me. This young woman and the person she called her pen pal are still trapped in something far beyond anything I can untangle on my own. I need to know whether readers, investigators, or anyone else willing to take this seriously can help bring some kind of peace to these souls. There may still be a way to free them from Candle Face's lair.

This is the first time I can remember hearing of Candle Face reaching beyond Central Texas, at least based on what I have gathered so far. But even that remains uncertain. The spirits don't come to me in the same order as Candle Face encountered them. The thought that her power may be spreading scares me more than almost anything else. Stay alert, and if you know something that may help, share it.

CANDLE FACE VICTIM #27: 'I LOVE YOU'

April 25, 2024

It had been six days since my last nocturnal visitor. These late-night encounters have pulled me back into a more familiar kind of fear. At least I had a short break. That ended this morning.

I was settling onto the couch, ready to fall asleep, when I saw the shadow in the far corner of the living room grow larger. My heart started pounding. I remember thinking, here we go again. I took a breath and waited for the spirit to show himself.

A young man in his early to mid-twenties stepped forward, draped in a sheet. I met his eyes and stayed quiet, letting him know I was listening. He took that as his cue and began to tell me what happened.

I left my apartment in San Marcos and headed toward my parents' place near Houston. I put their address into my GPS and left late in the evening, hoping to avoid the Christmas traffic. I took Highway 80. Near Stairtown, I saw a man standing on the side of the road in a construction vest and hard hat. He was holding a large white sign over his head that said, "CONTINUE STRAIGHT," with a black arrow pointing forward. He waved as I drove by. He looked like a road worker directing traffic, even though there was no construction anywhere around him.

A few minutes later, I passed a woman in a construction vest and hard hat holding a sign that read, "KEEP GOING, YOU'RE ALMOST THERE." She waved, and I honked back. By then, my GPS signal had dropped, so I had to rely on memory, and I had only driven that route twice before.

At the point where Highway 80 and Highway 183 meet, I saw another woman holding a sign with an arrow pointing straight ahead. I hesitated because I thought I needed to turn right, but she pointed straight at me and told me to keep going. I did. As I passed, she shouted, "I love you!" I laughed and honked again.

At another intersection, I saw a group standing there, each holding a sign. One of them stood out to me. It read, "BEYOND THIS PATH LIES THE UNKNOWN. TRUST YOUR HEART TO LEAD YOU HOME." It felt like the kind of prank my college friends would set up if they knew I was coming through.

That made me relax. I even sped up a little. Then I saw three friends from school standing by the road, waving signs that said, "YOU MADE IT," "WELCOME HOME," and "I LOVE YOU." Suddenly, they jumped in front of my car. I swerved to avoid them and slid to a stop on a dirt road. I jumped out into the glare of my headlights.

"What are ya'll doing here?"

They only laughed. Then they rushed me, grabbed my arms, and started steering me toward a barbed wire fence.

"Where are we going?"

"We're going to a party, and you're the guest of honor," they said. But their voices sounded hollow.

I hesitated. "Wait. I need to know where we're going before I go any farther."

"Don't be a baby. We love you," they said, laughing again.

That was when every instinct in me said something was wrong. I took a step back toward the fence. "I think I should go back to my car," I said, trying to sound calm.

Then their faces changed. Their bodies stretched and twisted until the three people I knew were gone. In their place were tall, black, swirling shadows hovering just above the ground. The air around us turned hot.

One of them came closer. It looked almost human, but too long, too warped, like a reflection pulled out of shape. When it spoke, the voice was smooth, calm, and worse because of it.

"This isn't a request."

Then it turned its head toward an old structure buried deep in the brush, almost hidden from sight.

The shadows stripped me naked and dragged me toward the house. It sagged under the weight of age, its windows dark and empty.

"Come," the shadow said. "She is waiting for you."

I tried to resist. "No. I need to go." But they ignored me. They pushed me through the door. Inside, the floor creaked under every step like old bones. The heat was suffocating. Every breath I took felt hotter than the one before, and the air smelled like decay and earth.

Dozens of candles lined the room. Their flames lit the shadows and guided me toward the center.

Then the room started to glitter, and Candle Face stepped out of the dark.

The stories made her sound like a pretty little girl. What I saw was tall, thin, her wax-like face lit softly by candlelight. Her hollow eye sockets seemed to look straight through me.

Her brow tightened. "I am irate," she said, her voice carrying through the room. "You refuse to believe in me. After all I have done, after all my efforts, your doubt has worn my patience thin."

The air grew hotter with every word.

I tried to speak. I wanted to apologize. I wanted to beg. But fear locked my throat.

"You will not ignore me any longer," she said.

With one motion of her hand, the floorboards gave way beneath me. I dropped and landed hard under the house.

As my eyes adjusted, I saw that I wasn't alone. Dozens of others were down there with me. Their eyes were hollow, but all of them seemed fixed on me. Together, they began to sing, over and over:

"I love you."

I lay there trapped under the floorboards while Candle Face kept speaking. She wasn't finished with me.

"One day, someone will come looking for you. Someone who loves you," she said. Then she laughed as her voice faded.

The silence after that was crushing, thick with the smell of old earth. I could feel the other spirits around me, each trapped in a nightmare of their own, each buried with a story nobody had heard.

Then her voice came again.

"It is not merely to torment you that I bind you here. There is a way out, a puzzle that, if solved, will break the chains that hold you here."

A faint light appeared above me, as if the idea of escape alone was enough to change the dark.

"Listen well," she said. "This riddle is your only key. The one who truly understands the power of this house can unravel it and free you."

The air grew hotter again. Then she gave me the riddle.

After that, silence returned. But now it carried the smallest possibility that someone might come, solve it, and get me out of there. Who that person is, I don't know. The answer is trapped in that house, the same as I am.

He stayed near the edge of the portal, gave me a tired grin, and turned to leave.

"Wait!" I shouted, louder than I meant to. The force of my own voice startled both of us. He turned back, his eyes wide, and I knew right away I had crossed a line again. Candle Face had warned me not to speak directly to the Lost Souls, and I had done it anyway.

Since I had already broken the rule, I kept going.

"What's the riddle? What did Candle Face tell you? If you want my help, then help me. Give me the riddle."

He glanced nervously back toward the portal, then looked at me like he thought he had nothing left to lose.

"She asked this," he said.

Across the cemetery's silent stones,
'I love you' pierces through the bones.
Who hears this declaration low,
where none but departed souls may go?

Then he turned back toward the portal. He looked torn for a second, until a calm but firm voice came from inside it.

"Come."

He gave a small nod and disappeared into the dark.

Personal Note to My Readers

I wrote the riddle down as fast as I could and rushed to my computer to record the rest of his testimony. I still don't know what it means.

Across the cemetery's silent stones,
'I love you' pierces through the bones.
Who hears this declaration low,
where none but departed souls may go?

There's a strange pattern here. "I love you" keeps showing up on the signs, in the voices of the fake construction workers, among the spirits under the house, and inside the riddle itself. I don't yet understand how those words connect to his death.

I searched online for clues and found nothing useful. I thought about asking the paranormal community, but too many of them seem more interested in dust specks and camera glitches than real hauntings. I may need to go there myself. It's less than two hours away. After thirty years in intelligence and investigations, I should trust my own methods enough to work this through.

I'll let you know what I find.

TO BE CONTINUED...

    We close this first volume of *Candle Face Chronicles: The Lost Souls*, knowing the investigation isn't over. So far, we have documented the deaths of twenty-seven victims, and I don't believe that is the end of it.

Night after night, spirits come into my house carrying another story. These restless souls have chosen me to speak for them, hoping someone will finally hear what happened to them. As I record each account, I keep hoping I'm getting closer to understanding the larger scope of Candle Face's power and finding some way to free those trapped in her lair.

To everyone who has stayed with me through this first volume, thank you. Your time, attention, and effort have already helped identify four Lost Souls in this book alone. The investigation is far from finished. Candle Face is still there, and there are likely many more waiting for someone to listen and try to help them.

If more Lost Souls come to me, I'll continue in a new volume, *Candle Face Chronicles: The Lost Souls [Book Two]*. There's still more to uncover. Each story adds another piece to the larger pattern and helps us better understand the death and suffering tied to Candle Face.

Until then, stay alert. Keep looking. And don't forget that more souls are likely still waiting to be heard. Their peace, and maybe some part of ours, depends on whether we keep going.

To be continued...

THANK YOU!

Thank you for reading *Candle Face Chronicles: The Lost Souls [Book One]*. I appreciate the time you spent reading this book. If you found it worthwhile, I'd be grateful if you took a few minutes to leave a review on Amazon (https://amzn.to/4bsM6ib). Even a short review helps. Reviews help a book find new readers, and I always appreciate hearing from readers. More readers mean a better chance of helping the Lost Souls.

Arthur M. Mills, Jr.

FOLLOW CANDLE FACE CHRONICLES ONLINE

- **Website: https://www.candleface.com**
  The central archive for the *Candle Face Chronicles* investigation.

- **Facebook: https://www.facebook.com/candlefacechronicles**
  Updates, findings, reader responses, and broader paranormal content beyond the core investigation.

- **YouTube: https://www.youtube.com/@CandleFace666**
  Video entries, readings, and case analysis.

- **Reddit: https://www.reddit.com/user/CandleFaceChronicles**
  A place for readers to help identify the Lost Souls, protect the Fugitives, and study Candle Face.

- **Medium: https://candlefacechronicles.medium.com**
  Longer journal entries and written case notes, often layered with clues.

NOTES

Keeping notes helps preserve details that might otherwise slip away. It's one of the best tools we have in the fight against Candle Face and in helping the Lost Souls who come to us for peace. A word, an observation, a location, or a piece of a spirit's story may help identify who they were, where their remains lie, or how Candle Face works.

Notes also help us track patterns, compare testimonies, and decide what to examine next. They let us honor the trust these spirits place in us by making sure their stories are recorded with care. As you take notes, return to the "Guiding Questions for the Lost Souls" at the beginning of the book. Use them to study each testimony more closely and to test your own ideas as the pattern grows.

If you want to compare ideas with other readers and share what you find, visit candleface.com. Working together gives us a better chance of finding answers and helping the Lost Souls still waiting for peace.

NOTES

NOTES

NOTES

NOTES

NOTES

NOTES

www.ingramcontent.com/pod-product-compliance
Lightning Source LLC
Chambersburg PA
CBHW070930180626
46817CB00003B/1224